subspace

Stuart Stromin

Columbus, Ohio
empbooks.com

First Edition: 6 10 12 15 19 22 24 33 11 1973
ISBN: 979-8-88596-190-5
LOC: 2024934015
Design, Layout, and Edits: Ezhno Martín
Cover: Dino Archon
Hieroglyph: Mooshe Nickerson

subspace

stories by
Stuart Stromin

Acknowledgments

"The Disciple"   First published in
                  Summer Fling *(Zimbell
                  House Publishing)*

"The Hat"   First published in
                  Here Comes Everyone
                  and in **HST** *(Horror
                  Sleaze Trash)*

"The Ditch"   First published in
                  Sin: Death of a Soul
                  (Macabre Ladies)

"Pindick"   First published online
                  in **HST** *(Horror Sleaze
                  Trash)* and in print
                  in **Dark Carnival**
                  (Macabre Ladies) and
                  Prose in Poor Taste.

Contents

subspace

(for G)

Come on in, the water's fine. The silvery water is cool and refreshing under the moonlight. Come in for a swim. Like hot cinders in an iron grate, you can see the city lights from the roof of the penthouse. We are in the shadows, you and I, surrounded by the glow of lamps in apartments and offices from the high buildings. The music from hidden speakers masks the rumble of the traffic below. The rooftop pool is surrounded by lush plants and hedgerows, like the garden of a mansion. I am swimming naked in the water.

There is a nude woman in the deep alleyway. Now she is gone. She appeared for just a moment illuminated by passing headlights in the inky shadows of the skyscrapers. She crosses the bathroom, leaving the door ajar. She gets out of the shower, and takes a towel from the metal rack. She knows that I am peeping through the hinge crack in the door. She covers up waist-down, but leaves her breasts exposed, as she bends forward. Firm, they dangle like forbidden fruit, as she raises up.

We have done this before.

Now I am on my knees, my head bowed, my hands behind my back. She walks past on the way to her mirror, and the glass shelf where her palette of make-up vials and powders wait. She brushes past me, without looking at me, and I feel her palm smack the back of my head. It is just a tease. It is a message between us. A communiqué is delivered across the battleground.

Far beneath our rooftop refuge, the sirens of ambulances and patrol cars scream through the city.

She has dipped a toe into the cool water, flicked it along the surface. She takes the temperature.

She is reading me. She is circling me. She moves like a predator. She is trying to gauge where I am, who I am now. I am not the same man who walked through the door. I have relinquished my importance. I have unbuttoned my white shirt, I have loosened my tie. I am a man without a suit. I wear nothing but the vague scent of my cologne. I purchased the expensive cologne at the duty free store at the airport, presenting my passport and boarding pass to the pair of salesgirls with perfect lipstick. I am on a journey. I try to forget everything about the day, about the grind and conflict of the day, about the problems I will face tomorrow. She too has a lot to forget. She has to forget her own legacy, and the thousand ways that history has abused her. She stares at me in the mirror, and there is the glare of eye contact between us, but I lower my eyes. I dare not meet her gaze. I wait. We are waiting. We are going to do something. There will be violence.

The violence is part of the trust. We are in a dance of trust, intimate, vulnerable, and to the edge of danger. We are performing a ceremony, like a religious ritual, or a marriage.

I am splashing back and forth in the lap pool, like a prisoner pacing a cell. The water is a perfect temperature to soothe the summer night. I kick my legs. I swim as fast as I can go to feel the tired muscles ache.

I hear the thunder of a whip crack. A warm-up. A warning.

Come on in. We have done this before. It has strengthened us, and liberated us. It has confounded us and made as feel the shame of lust and recklessness.

There is a grubby pervert in a vertical box, rubbing away in his own imaginary frenzy. He is in an old-fashioned English telephone booth, making a dirty telephone call from his narrow, red cage. He cannot control his breathing, or his slobbering, or what his hands and fingers do by themselves. He dials numbers, listening to the whir as the dial finds its way back home.

There is a woman intoxicated. The faint hint of alcohol lingers. She likes the taste of it, she likes the way it makes her feel. It is an old friend, it smoothes the old creaks and plains.

We are witnesses to one another's vulnerability. This is how we look when we are defenseless. There is no pretense. I am a man who has actualized his fantasies. I am a man who has had the ability to wield my devious imagination into flesh and blood. There are a lot of men like me; we all find a way to demand reality. I have committed every act of debauchery that my fiendish mind could conceive. She is a willing participant, and a wicked contributor in our creative carnality. She wants to see all the way down this tunnel to the light.

She does not want to harm me, but she has signed her name in welts and bruises. She can be rough in her handling. There are always scars. There is always the residue of experience on the road to transcendence. There is ash after the fire.

Where is your evil twin? She has been missing for some time, but I am confident that she is alive and well. She is in hiding. She has escaped, through some spooned out tunnel, or a wormhole into a mysterious dimension. She has left a trail of crusty breadcrumbs through the forest. She will return for me. She has promised to return. She knows that - if I were on the run - I would come back for her.

I would not leave her alone.

I am not a runaway, but I am a runner. I am not fast, but I can turn invisible. This is a useful skill when one is on the run. I have been on the run before. If I were ever on the run again, I would come back for her.

The only reason I would not come back is if she were the one who chased me off.

This is my testament, if you want to hear it. This is my confession, now that all the truths must come out, like liquid seeping from a net, where the fish lie flapping. All truths come out, even to the last breath.

There is no truth like fantasy. In fantasy, there are myths and archetypes, heroes and seductresses, helpless victims and inventive tormenters, palace and dungeon; there are those childhood fears and fascinations, the dreams and imagery of lost imaginations; the twisted scenarios, and the throb of primal sexual and brutal lust for gratification; and, in fantasy, when it is all laid bare, there is catharsis.

She is sitting beneath a folded umbrella on the other side of the pool. The skeletal umbrella is like a bird perched with its wings clenched. There is a breeze now. The water is getting cold. She is huddled in the shadows, wrapped up in a towel or blanket, like a cloak figure. She is backstage, she has not yet made her entrance. She is watching me, swimming naked in the long pool, but she is disinterested. She is not coming.

Your evil twin is not coming back for me. She is free now, she is on the run.

Once you were gone, it was never the same. It has never been the same. The core of the sun is dark. There is an intensity that used to be there, where I was and where you were; it is blind in this place.

On the clammy black walls, there are a thousand colors shimmering.

You will be able to go wherever your imagination takes you. We are trespassing on this terrain. Wild animals do not respect the boundaries.

I am on my back now. I am relaxing in the water. I am floating in the naked water. I spread my arms, Christ-like. I am nailed to a liquid cross. I float on the surface, my face exposed although my ears are underwater. I hear the singing of the filter and the jets. I shut my eyes. I am in my own sensory deprivation, in the tepid water. I cannot hear if you were to speak. You do not speak. You hold your silence, but the voices in your head are deafening. You are confused by the voices in your mind. There are so many permutations. Topsy-turvy. I float, bobbing beneath the water, face up, eyes closed. I am so vulnerable. My face is above the surface, naked genitals peeping through a hole in the water. I am shivering, everything is shriveled. To her, I seem so powerless and so grateful, like a sacrifice pinned on the water.

I drift face down like a dead man. I am a drowned man. I am a hanged man. I am a corpse in a horizontal box, with no work or pleasure or intimacy.

Can this be true? Can anything be true? Do I dare? Do I dare? Do I dare?

I dare you.

Come and get me. You know where I am, and you know how to find me. You have found me before. You know the pathways, although I have disguised them with brambles and with thistle. I have laid false clues. I have doubles, dressed in my costumes. I have changed the map to my house. But you will find me in my secret hideaway. Your instincts guide you. You have found your way there before.

Come on in, the water's fine.

The Dress

(for Christina)

By the time Frank got back to the suite from the convention floor, Valentina was already in the hotel.

A group of her friends had offered her a ride to Las Vegas on the bumpy back roads from Palm Springs in a dusty purple convertible. They were all dressed in leather, with exotic piercings and tattoos. An orange sun was falling slowly over the mountains on the horizon. They smoked pot on the way, and the journey through the desert left her in a state of bliss and beauty.

Bliss and beauty were her natural state, if ignorance was bliss and beauty was skin deep. Inked along her arm in a flourish of peacock colors - turquoise, emerald, amber - was a lavish bouquet of patterns that looked so much like flowers that combined with her perfume, it often attracted bees. She lived in morbid fear of being mistaken for a garden and getting stung.

She was never without her smart phone, in its shiny case, and she texted Frank when her friends dropped her off at his hotel. With her left arm extended so you could see the sleeve tattoo, Valentina took a picture of herself under the marquee standing next to the porter and the gold-plated luggage cart. The rest of her group was staying at the cheap motel under the neon sign across the street, but they already knew they would all be hanging out in his suite at the four-star resort when the night drifted into the small hours.

As promised, there was a key waiting in the pocket of a small, square envelope for her at the reception desk. On a high level, the suite overlooked the Strip on a cloudy winter day. There was a Las Vegas-sized bed, and two flat-screen tvs, and a bathroom with mirrored walls. She unpacked her lilac-and-leopard bag and undressed and began to get ready for the night.

They were all in town for the awards, and the first thing that she had to do in good time for the glittering event on Saturday night was to get a dress.

That was where he came in.

When he opened the door of the suite, Frank was still wearing his suit and tie, which always made him look more handsome, with his soft hair brushed back, and a confident step after his successful day at the convention. She could tell that he did not know what to expect.

What he got was a pleasant surprise.

She was waiting at the door, so he saw her to her full effect, as soon as he entered. She had practiced a mesmerizing gaze. She was wearing a wig, with long dark tresses to match her limpid eyes. Her makeup was flawless, with full red lips, and smoky eye-shadow. Pink latex lingerie hugged the curves of her body, and black stockings with a pink latex garter swept down her legs to her black spiky heels.

Frank smiled, lingering coyly behind the door, before stepping into the room. As he shut the door, he hung the do not disturb sign around the door-handle.

She was upon him with hardly a hello, pulling on his tie and his buttons.

They had not seen each other in a while, and she wasted no time in devouring him. It all happened so suddenly, and suddenly therefore, it was over. She did everything he loved and wanted - still managing to hold back a little tease - with such a ravenous passion that they moved through the motions at a fierce tempo.

He could not say she had not performed to her utmost, and he was satisfied that the weekend had got off to such a promising start. Suspense only created tension. She had wasted no time in cutting to the chase.

There was a lot to do still, and the night was falling.

"I have to get ready," she said, as they lay on the sheets staring up at the mirrored ceiling, but - transfixed by her own perfect counterpart directly above her - she did not move.

"Do you want to grab some dinner?" he offered, "I'm starving."

"Yes, we'll eat, but first, we have to get the dress." She crawled naked over his naked body, her firm round breasts brushing against his stomach, and clambered off the bed. "For the awards on Saturday night."

He grinned, because he understood what the unspoken deal between them was, and Valentina had already taken care of her share of the bargain. "I promised I would get you a dress. Don't worry. We'll go shopping."

"Yay." She clapped her palms with her fingertips arched, and gave him a big exaggerated kiss on the cheek. "You're so sweet."

She went into the bathroom, leaving the door ajar so that he could watch her in the shower, as the soapy water spilled over her body. Sometimes, she showered five or six times in a day. She knew he was feasting his eyes on her and, she took a long time to wash, enjoying the hot foamy water and the steam.

They went to the Forum, the upscale shopping center attached to Caesar's Palace. The long elevators curved in a luxurious arc beneath a ceiling painted blue. The casino played tricks with the light. You could not tell what was real and what was illusion. Facades of old buildings contained modern stores with famous brands set in a maze of alleys. It seemed that they were walking through an old European town, on a summer afternoon. There were fountains in cobblestone squares, which were replicas of actual piazzas in Italy. Artificial sunlight streamed down onto the busy cafes and bars and boutiques.

He kept trying to steer her towards the restaurants. "I have to eat something," he said, looking at a chalk menu posted on a blackboard on the terrace, "I was on the convention floor and in meetings all day. I never had lunch."

"Let's just get the shopping finished, so we don't have to stress through dinner. All we need is the dress and the shoes."

"The shoes?"

"We need the shoes to go with the dress."

"Well, I don't have that much cash on me."

"Credit card," Valentina suggested.

"You don't want to hear about the credit cards," Frank groaned, rolling his eyes, "Trust me."

"Well then, I hope you brought enough money. Sometimes the shoes cost more than the dress."

His palms grew a little clammy, and he had to let go of her fingers, so that he could wipe his hand on his pocket.

They went into the first store, and a woman in her forties, who looked and sounded

Middle Eastern, came to serve them. This was Valentina's turf, and he knew better than to interfere. There was a bank of comfortable armchairs - just for men like him - and he sat down and sank into the soft cushions. There were no other customers in the store. Valentina and the saleslady started working their way through the racks, paging through the garments like the leaves of a catalog.

They disappeared into the changing rooms with an armful of clothes. He stood up on the plush carpet, and, in an off-hand way, he sauntered over to the rack, where he began leafing through the dresses himself, trying to find not an outfit but a price tag. There were no prices on anything, and he started to feel panicky.

Valentina emerged. The dress looked like it was made of macramé with splotches of silver, the way expensive restaurants grate truffles over plain macaroni and cheese to increase the price. She paced up and down, as if she were on the runway for him, and twirled around so that he could absorb the full impact.

"What do you think?" she asked.

He frowned. "Let me see one of the others."

"He doesn't like it," she said to the saleslady, "I can tell from his face." Without so much as a pout, she marched back to the changing room.

"How much is that dress?" he asked, as casually as he could, when she was out of earshot.

"Let me see," the saleslady answered, "That's fourteen ninety five. So, say, fifteen hundred dollars."

He turned instantly pale, and broke into a cold sweat. He had to go and sit down in the armchair again to catch his breath. He felt a slight dizziness, probably because he needed food. Valentina came marching out again, with a costume change, although the second dress looked much the same as the first.

"This one is much cheaper," offered the saleslady, "Its only nine hundred. And it looks beautiful on her."

"Well, every dress looks beautiful on her. She's a beautiful woman. But we are buying a dress for a special occasion, and you know, this dress is not right for the occasion."

"What kind of dress would be right for the occasion?" asked the lady from the store.

"We need something flashy."

"You don't think this is flashy enough?"

"I like the dress," Valentina volunteered, but she did not seem convinced of her own opinion.

"Honey, you got to think about what all those other girls will be wearing. This dress doesn't look - well, how should I say it - it's not sexy enough."

"You know what?" Valentina nodded. "You're right."

"I have lots of other dresses. Sexy ones."

"I don't know if we will find the dress in this store," he said, mostly to Valentina.

She took his side. "We need something more revealing. Something that shows some leg. Or some cleavage."

"Exactly," he agreed. "Let's look around. This is only the first store. We can always come back, if we don't find anything else."

When they walked out of the store, she took his arm, and said, "You know, I didn't like that store."

Much relieved, he agreed. "That's an old lady store. Let's find something that works for you."

The store which was for the young and beautiful was part of a national chain, and there were young customers and a young saleswoman, with a nose ring, who mouthed along with the lively music on the speakers.

As soon as they walked in, Valentina slipped a dress off the first rack. It was sparkling and sleek, with a plunging neckline, and dotted with sequins.

"What do you think of this one?" she held up the hanger.

The price tag dangled in front of him. It read one hundred and four dollars.

"I love it," he said, trying to contain his enthusiasm.

"Me too," she said, as they ventured deeper into the store.

They began to look around, and, as all the dresses were similar, in style and pricing, they both began to realize how much they liked the merchandise, and how much they preferred the sexy young store to the old lady store. With his encouragement, Valentina selected a total of four dresses from the racks to take to the changing room. The other dresses were each priced at one hundred and twenty dollars.

Valentina came prancing out of the changing room, with a spring in her step, and the first dress, which cost one hundred and four dollars, hugging the curves of her body.

"I love this dress," she pronounced, with a gleam in her eye.

"You look sensational."

She made a pirouette. "It fits so well."

"It's sexy and it's classy."

She spun about and started back towards the changing room, but then stopped. "I don't want to take it off. I don't really need to try on any of the other ones, do I?"

"We've found it," he agreed, "We've found the dress."

"Now," she said, "All we need are the shoes."

He carried the package with her old dress from the store, as they resumed their journey through the mall in search of a shoe store. Valentina skipped past the shop windows, staring with delight at her reflection in the new dress, and also, on the prowl for shoes.

Frank wanted to eat first, especially because everything was becoming more crowded. He hated standing in a line, and his stomach was growling. He almost succeeded in navigating Valentina into a French bistro, but they came upon a shoe store.

In the window, under spotlights, there were shoes on plastic stands, in a display of sparkles and shimmer, but - again - no price tags.

Arm-in-arm, Valentina pulled him into the store, and, sitting beside him on a narrow stool, tried on a pair of pumps.

"They fit perfectly," she proclaimed.

"How much are these shoes?" he asked the salesman.

"Fifteen hundred."

"For the pair?" he made sure.

"Yes, we always sell them as a pair."

"I really like how they fit." Valentina strutted up and down in front of a ground-level mirror tilted forward to showcase the footwear. "And they are really sexy."

"Yes," he said, experiencing a moment of déjà vu, "But the problem is that they don't go with the dress. If you wear those shoes, they will really clash with the dress."

"You're right," she said, "Let's try somewhere else."

They went to a different store, and found a pair of shoes for ninety-nine dollars, which fit perfectly, and was an ideal combination for the dress. They both thought how lucky it was that they had not taken the first selection she had tried. After he finished paying, he took a photograph of her with her smart phone. Valentina was so delighted with the purchases that she insisted on wearing the full outfit, while he carried her earlier items in the shopping bags for the latest.

Frank was momentarily disheartened, when Valentina led him into a perfume store, but all she wanted was a splash of scent from the tester on the counter, now that there was no jeopardy of being pursued by any swarms.

Both satisfied with the progress of the evening, they finally turned their attention to dinner, but wherever they looked, the restaurants were packed.

"Sushi?" she suggested which she knew was his favorite.

"We can try. But I don't think we'll get a table now."

They crossed the cobblestones of the Italian plaza to the Japanese restaurant, with rice-paper lanterns, and waitresses in kimonos. She waited on the cobblestones under the shifting colors of the casino roof, and caught up on her text messages, while Frank, carrying the shopping bags, went to the desk to ask for a table.

A platinum blonde hostess looked at him with a blank expression. "We're booked solid."

"There are only two of us."

"With the awards tomorrow," she sniffed, "You need a reservation a month in advance."

"How long if we wait?"

"I'm sorry. We won't have a table for three and a half hours."

Appearing like a presence, at that moment, Valentina glided up beside him, exuding beauty in the clinging new dress and the matching footwear. The vivid tattoo snaked along her arm. Her eyes glowered through smoky shadow.

"We'd like to eat now," she uttered.

The hostess surrendered entirely. "Right this way."

The Hat

(for Rosa)

Samira forgot the hat the first time, so he had to go back to see her again. Except for the absence of the hat, it had been fine the first time. She had done everything the way she always did it, with the murmur of her crisp accent, and the glare of her blue eyes. It still felt like there was something missing somehow, and, when Leon left her little room and went down the steep, twisted staircase, and into the brisk air of the street, and the glow of the red lights against the gloom of the night, he realized what it was. She had forgotten to wear the hat.

It was not the same without the hat.

She called it a hat, because her English was limited, but it was really a cap. It was made of black rubber, kept to a dull shine, with a wide latex peak and a sharp crown molded to a soft point at the crest. There was a white latex band that ran around it in a thin stripe. It fit snugly on her head, making her seem even taller, over six-foot in spiky heels, with her golden hair streaming, and her gimlet blue eyes gazing from beneath the peak.

Leon had bought her the hat on a business trip one year. He had not been looking for a hat, but he was looking for a gift. When he saw the hat, Leon knew immediately that it was what he wanted for her. She loved the hat, when she received it, although she loved anything if it was a present. There was no such thing as a disappointing gift. Leon never arrived empty-handed. He brought her designer jeans, perfume, inexpensive jewelry, t-shirts from his travels, and once, for her young son, a toy train.

From the first time that Samira wore the hat for him, it became part of her costume. It matched her long latex boots, and her long black gloves, and her golden locks brushing her shoulders. It went with the exposed girders, splintery rafters and hanging chains and the smell of wax in the dim light of the room. They heard the raucous noise of the passers-by, drunken singing outside, and accordion music from a nearby bar. He sometimes gulped down a stiff shot of vodka there, before he knocked on her door. He did not want to feel like himself, he wanted to hide behind intoxication when they played out their ritual.

They had to do everything again from the beginning - with the hat this time - when he went back the next night.

She had a short crop, and she strutted up and down upon the mat, stopping with her face nose-to-nose right in his face, and her riding crop teasing across his unclothed body. He felt the heat rising from her, and there was a sweet, musk scent when she was close to him.

She exuded a commanding presence. She barked orders and made him march naked from wall to wall with one hand swinging at his side, and the other hand clutching his genitals.

"I am the Kommandant," she insisted, tucking the crop under her arm, "Left, right! Left, right! Left, right!"

"Yes, Kommandant!"

"I decide what is good, and what is not good," she said ominously.

"Good, good, good," he pleaded, "I am good."

"If you are not good, you know what will happen to you," she warned.

His eyes filled up with terror, and she smiled wickedly.

He always felt such a cathartic sense of relief when it was all over, as if she had done him an enormous favor by filling a desperate need.

She took the hat off, indicating that they were finished, and she could not wait to get out of the boots and back into her walking shoes and her street clothes. He got dressed one button at a time with his back to her, so that they did not have to look at one another.

Afterwards, they sometimes went for dinner together in Chinatown. There was a place where the ducks were hanging in the window on S-shaped hooks, and they shared a lemony dish with hot oysters on the half-shell. They drank sweet beer served in chilled tankards. She spoke to the waiter in a guttural language that he could not understand. From the restaurant, they could see the barges floating down the canals and the colored lights from the district reflecting on the ripples of the water. They heard the peal of the bells chiming the hour from the Old Church, as it grew later, but they lingered over the meal. Neither of them had anywhere in particular to go, and the kitchen stayed open until midnight.

The square tables were close together, and the people beside them could overhear their conversation, but they kept everything innocent. They had known each other for many years, and, like old friends, they talked and joked about everything under the moon, except the taboo of what had just occurred between them in her room. Now, after the fact, when it had worn off for both of them, what they had done seemed traumatic and depraved. It felt like they had committed a crime. They had a familiar aftertaste that lingered from the time they did it before until the time that they would do it again. They were not ashamed, but there was a grubby feeling that stained them on the inside. She never wanted to speak about it; for her, it was work, and the dinner was personal.

There was only one other subject that they never talked about, and that was what had happened to his family. It was a long time ago, and besides, that was in another country.

The Shoes and The Boots

(for Olivia)

Captain Otto Ledyak was a disgusting specimen. He had a pocky, misshapen face with a bulbous nose pricked with carbuncles and whiskers, and a podgy frame. His hair was like gray straw. He had bad teeth and foul-smelling breath, as a result of a diet rich in pickles and garlic. The unattractiveness of the officer was counter-matched in equal degree only by the radiant beauty of Irena, who worked in his offices, and interacted with the captain on a daily basis. She had fiery eyes, thick hair, and a tender body without a blemish. To her own revulsion, she found herself uncannily drawn to him in the most shocking ways.

She witnessed him in action at the bureau. He was not sympathetic. He was shrewd and lordly, and he relished the superiority of command in a way that was apparent. It was not so much a sense of arrogance as self-assuredness, even though he had attained his rank through family connections. Whatever it was about his swagger, she was hideously attracted to it, and, despite herself, longed to fall under his spell.

On the one hand, she could not imagine anything more revolting to her, because she was generally of a reserved disposition derived from a natural shyness, but, on the other hand, the sheer vulgarity of being at his carnal beck was fiendishly arousing to her.

He was not devoid of charm, but there was no way to get beyond his troll-like appearance. In addition, there was a body odor about him, as if here was a man who had resolved to make himself as odious to the world as possible. All with whom he interacted attempted to maintain a formal personal distance beyond their olfactory ranges.

Irena likewise tried to avoid him as much as possible, although she was always observing him from a distance as if she were drawn to his aura by a magnet. The captain, when he engaged with her, examined her with a penetrating eye and was always familiar and disdainful.

One day, passing her work desk in the outer lobby, he made an unkind comment about her shoes.

"You know, it would be better if you went around in bare feet than with those scuff marks on your shoes," he said off-handedly.

She flushed and lowered her eyes. "I will see that it doesn't happen again."

"Once upon a time, those were very acceptable shoes," he condescended, "But they are used and worn. You need new shoes. I will buy them for you."

She did not know what to make of the comment or the conversation or the promise to pay for the shoes. The next day, she wore a different pair of shoes, even though they were not much better in repair, and no more was said about anything. Irena thought it best to let the matter drop and she tried to stay out of his way at the department, where there were many other co-workers.

But, after a few weeks, he suddenly blurted, "Well, Irena, I must be true to my word."

She looked at him, uncertain of how to respond. "Yes, captain, of course."

"I mean about the shoes."

"Oh, you don't have to give me any money," she held up her hand.

"No, of course not," he said, "I will take you shopping. I know just the establishment where they have the very best of shoes, and also, I need a new pair of boots. So, we will go together tomorrow afternoon, and you will have new shoes. As was my word."

This was - of course - his command, and there was no choice but to obey it. She lowered her eyes in subordination, and caught the little grin at the side of his mouth, as he savored his moment of authority. She felt a tingle of excitement in her loins.

In the night, she lay in her bed, fantasizing about the sway he held, and the dirtiness of succumbing to the control of such a repulsive character. Under the blue light of the moon, which poured through her bedroom window, she writhed in her bed sheets, whispering nasty words and calling herself the vilest names. Asleep, she dreamed of uniformed soldiers marching on a frosty parade ground, and she woke to an overcast day, feeling rested and alert.

It was Saturday, so she would not see him until they met at the boutique in the late afternoon. In the winter, the sun set early and there were rain clouds gathering when she arrived for the rendezvous. Beneath her coat, she was wearing a loose dress that hugged the curves of her body. She was wearing her old shoes - the ones he had objected to - because she planned to discard them when she received the new shoes.

From the outside, it was easy to see into the store where it was warm and well lit, with upholstered furniture for the select group of clientele. In the windows, and through the windows, along the shelves, there were many rich displays of different footwear for men and women.

The captain was already in the boutique, sitting in a round-backed chair, with his legs stretched out in his brand new boots. Attending him, there was a well-dressed young man from the shoe store, with buckteeth which gave him a perpetual smile.

"I'm Maurice," said the well-dressed man, "Please have a seat."

"Irena," she said, with a bow of her head and sat into the chair opposite the captain, following his motion.

"These are my new boots," said the captain, aiming his legs towards her, and swiveling the toes, "Weatherproof. Durable. The latest thing in the capital. What do you think?"

The boots were a dull black, the color and texture of a thick whip, and went a long way up his legs.

"Very impressive," she said.

"They could do with a polish," he said gruffly, with a look at Maurice. "But they're comfortable, that's what I care about it."

"Yes, of course, that's the main thing," she said, taking off her coat because it was heated in the store.

"Indeed." He looked her up and down from her clinging dress to her old shoes. "Well, tell him your size and he'll bring out your new shoes."

She was not sure what to say, when Maurice fell to his knees on the carpet, as if the shop assistant were about to ask for her hand in marriage, and began to remove her old shoes.

"Oh, my goodness," he said, sliding the first shoe from her foot, "What have we here? My dear, wait until you see what we have picked out for you."

He removed the other shoe, and, with each hand gave her bare feet a squeeze to stimulate the blood. Then, from beneath her chair, he brought out a wooden footstool onto which he placed her feet. There was a built-in measuring device to read the exact size of each foot by placing one heel at a time into the scoop of a holder fixed to a ruler with a sliding block which stopped against the toe.

Captain Ledyak leaned forward in his chair, studying as the precise measurements were taken. She saw that both men were staring at her feet, which were dainty and well-manicured, and she remembered the captain's remark in the office. She wriggled her toes, and, catching their reactions, she wriggled them again, and rotated her ankles. Oblivious to any other distractions, the men were focused on her naked feet.

The captain heaved a sigh, as if he were contemplating a natural wonder or a masterpiece of artwork, leaving a faint smell of onions which had been consumed with his lunch.

Maurice clambered back up off the floor, withdrew a notebook and a pencil from his pocket, and jotted down the sizes. "Let me get your new shoes."

He went to the other side of the counter, just as the first raindrops rattled against the shop windows.

The captain said, "You have very delicate feet."

She did not know how to respond, so she just twitched her feet again, and he kept staring at her toes, especially mesmerized by the big toe on the right foot.

Maurice came back with an embossed cardboard box and knelt in front of her again, humming a little fanfare to add to the anticipation.

Like a conjurer revealing the surprise of a vanished pigeon, he opened the lid and she saw the most beautiful and expensive shoes that she could have possibly imagined. Irena understood at that moment how profligate women accumulate vast shoe collections, as if they were hoarding treasure. Every detail was flawless. The leather was of the highest quality, with a luxurious sheen, and the cut was of an elegance beyond any venue where she might ever have use of it.

"This is too much," she said, embarrassed by the bounty.

"Nonsense," rebuked the captain, "You will have the shoes." It was his command, and there was that satisfied grin again at the corners of his lips.

"Yes, captain. Thank you, sir." She pressed her palms together in gratitude. "You are very generous."

Maurice slid the shoes onto her feet, one by one. "How do they fit?"

They were like slippers.

"Perfectly." Irena stood up.

"That's because I measured you myself,"

Maurice affirmed, with a buck-toothed smile. "People never know their own sizes."

"Go ahead," instructed the captain, with a wave of his arm, "Walk around."

The shoes felt so light on her feet, as she strutted around the store, and although Captain Ledyak did not move from his seat, his eyes followed her up and down wherever she moved. She twirled around, like a ballerina, with her hem lifting as she spun.

"Now, come and sit down again," the captain called, pointing with his finger as if he were instructing a dog.

She stopped her prancing, and immediately went to sit in the chair across from him. He did not look her in the eyes, his gaze was fixed lower.

"What do you think?" he demanded, "They fit well? Do you like them?"

"I don't know how to thank you."

"Maurice, put them on my bill. The shoes and the boots."

"Would you like me to box them for you?" asked the attendant.

The captain shook his head. "No, box the ones we came in. We'll wear the new stuff. Even though these boots could do with a polish."

"Yes, sir." Maurice gathered up all the old footwear.

"Do you have any polish?"

"I'll get you some polish at once." He dashed off to the back room.

Outside, the rain pelted down, smearing the view of the world through the misted windowpanes like the pastels of a runny watercolor painting.

"I must say you have some beautiful feet," said the captain, "Those shoes are an exquisite compliment to you."

"I like your boots," she blushed.

Maurice came scampering back with a full shoe-shining kit.

Once again, he sank to his knees, brush and polish in hand, about to buff the captain's boots.

"No, Maurice," said the captain, "Leave the brush. You go and box up the old shoes. She can do it."

Irena felt that twinge run through her again.

"Go ahead, Irena," the captain told her, pushing out his feet, "Polish my boots." He gave a little grin.

Irena got down onto the carpet like a peasant at his heels. Other patrons, browsing the shelves, noticed and tittered, but she complied as if she were entranced. She wiped a cloth across the boots first, feeling the stiffness of the warm, new leather. She cradled the brush in her hand, and it fit snugly. The smell of the polish was so strong to her that she could taste it. On her knees, she ran the brush over every detail of the boots. On each, she worked the toe, heel and all the way along the shaft up to the collar, where there was a filigree of metal beading. She stroked up and down, first gently with just the timid bristles of the brush teasing across the surface, and then in hard, rhythmic strokes, grinding all her force into it. She kept going without interruption. The captain was grunting with satisfaction and then gave a little splutter, and a line of saliva dribbled down the side of his mouth. He heaved a sigh, and wiped his lips with the back of his sleeve. Maurice came back with the old shoes, bundled up, and the receipt.

When they emerged from the store into the winter air, the sky was dark and the rain was steadily falling. There were few pedestrians out in the gloomy weather.

"I will walk you to the corner," the captain offered, "So, that you can share the cover of my umbrella."

They walked together some two dozen yards. Irena was carrying a package containing her old shoes, with her purse over her arm. She was careful to avoid stepping in any puddles. She was already thinking of occasions where she might have the opportunity to flaunt the stylish new shoes. The sparkling pair was already her prize possession. She stayed close to him to be better protected against the elements.

They reached the intersection of the road. In the gutters, there was a wash of muddy water flowing in the street. Choked with refuse and flotsam, the drains overflowed, bringing the fetor of excrement and offal. The currents, eddying and swirling, swelled as the sheets of rain filled the rushing stream like a bog. There was no way to cross without stepping into it.

"I am supposed to go left here," said Irena.

"I'm going right," said the captain with the umbrella.

"Perhaps, the captain could wait with me until the rain stops..."

"No, Irena," he grinned, with a thrust of his chin, "Walk across."

"But, I have..."

"You will not disobey me..." he ordered, with a cruel smirk.

She recognized the glint in his eye. "Yes, sir."

In blind obedience, Irena stepped out into the street, and the filthy gush of water immediately deluged her feet, and soaked her new shoes.

"Bravo, Irena!" laughed the captain.

By the time she made it to the other side of the road, she was drenched and the extravagant shoes were ruined. She took the shoes off and stood barefoot on the wet ground, while, beneath the shelter of his umbrella, the captain leered from the opposite bank. Fortunately, Maurice had boxed up the old shoes, so Irena put them back on her beautiful feet to make her way home.

That night, after the rain ceased and the clear, blue moonlight streamed through her window, she lay in bed quivering as she envisioned all the events of the afternoon.

On Monday at the office, she was visited by a very cultivated lady, wearing fine clothing, pearls and French perfume, whom she had never seen before.

The woman stood close to her work desk and inquired, "So, you're Irena?"

"Yes, madam."

"Well, you are a charming creature. And where are the new shoes?"

"The shoes?"

"Come on, my dear, it's no use pretending. He has confessed all. I know all about it. He came home in a state of rhapsody."

"I can not wear the new shoes," Irena explained, "They were all covered in muck after we left the store."

"I see. That must have been disappointing." She reached into her purse, and pulled out a handful of money. "Here. You will go back and replace them."

"Well, I couldn't accept..."

"It's the least I can do," insisted the woman, laying the amount on her desk, "You will not have to put up with this tomfoolery again. Now, where will I find my husband?"

Irena pointed out Captain's Ledyak's private office, and, even through the closed doors, everyone in the department could hear the woman berating him, and the plaint of his pathetic apologies as the officer dropped to his knees and begged for his wife's forgiveness.

The Necklace

(for Bettie)

Mia was nervous about going on a trip with Whitey, but she agreed to it, because basically she did not want to pay for a room, and because Whitey agreed to all of her conditions.

Number one, don't expect sex. He expected nothing, he promised, he just needed her as an armpiece to take to a business dinner, because let's face it, she was striking with her smoldering Latin looks - long, dark, curly hair, high cheekbones, almond eyes, full lips. Number two, she was traveling with two companions, both of whom, in different ways were trans, which was her crowd, being that she was mostly the L in LGBTQ. He said that he had a suite which held enough space for all, and that he just wanted company, and her friends were welcome. He said that the three of them could sleep in the bed, and he would sleep on the sofa in the living room.

That sounded sincere, and actually, his name was Wiley, but in her head she could not help thinking of him as Whitey.

Mia had faced so many bad experiences with privileged, condescending men of his ilk.

She was pleased that she was with Gina, and Terry, as chaperones, in case things went sour.

The hotel key was waiting as he had arranged, and when they got to the suite, he was not there, but had left them a gift basket and a bottle of champagne.

There was a king size hot tub in the room, and soon, they were all lounging around naked, drinking champagne.

They were having such a gratifying time that they hardly noticed when Wiley dropped into the tub naked to join them. He had brought more champagne, and everyone was in high spirits, and he turned out to be absolutely cool.

They were all fooling around with each other, in a kind of a flirty way, since they were all naked in the tub, after all. It was more playful than nasty, and he never crossed any lines, or got pushy, but it was clear that Wiley was enjoying being in the mix.

At one point, Gina decided to put some make up on him, and Wiley went into a swoon. She did his lips, and then to top it off, Mia put a necklace around his neck, which said in big gold italic letters: *Bitch*.

For the rest of the night - because they never left the suite - Wiley paraded around wearing nothing but lipstick and the necklace.

The next morning, after waking up early, he cleaned himself up, and got dressed up in his suit and tie to go to a meeting, and there he was again, like Whitey, like every man who had ever hounded or harassed her.

He must have seen her hackles raised, because he leaned in to her, and pulled aside his collar. Beneath his white shirt, he was still wearing the necklace. "Come on, Mia," he grinned, "I'm still your bitch."

The Bracelet

Sylvia Robles did not steal because she needed the money.

She had money, and she had always had money, first from her family, growing up with an ocean view in the Pacific Palisades, and then, she married it. She lived in an upscale house - anywhere else it would be a mansion - behind a high green hedge and at the end of a long driveway halfway up the canyon in Beverly Hills. Other than the money, her husband, Hector, a banker, was not interesting. He kept his nine to fives, and golfed on the weekend in cream-colored slacks, and never listened to a single word she said. That suited her fine, because whenever he had anything to say to her, he put her straight to sleep. Their entire marriage was lethargic. She lay in the feathery pillows of her four-poster bed in the morning with hardly a reason to get out of it. Sylvia was in such a malaise of ennui that she hardly knew she existed. She did not have a career, or need one, or want one. She did not have a hobby or any diversion that made her heart race. She did not steal for the money, she stole to feel alive.

It had started off, stealing from friends. She always had a veiled contempt for her friends. They were spoiled, self-centered bores, who thrived on trivial gossip. She wanted to take something from one of them, just to inflict an injury, to see if anyone would even notice. The first time she ever did it was quite by impulse. All the hens were at some tedious daytime affair, and she could not wait to get out of there as soon as she finished her tea. When she went to the guest closet for her jacket, she saw Elysia's jacket with its obnoxious sequins. Elysia was a lively spirit, a little younger than the rest of them, with a petite body and an annoying cackle, and she always wanted to be the center of attention. Without even thinking about it, Sylvia dipped her hand into the jacket pocket, and took out her wallet. She used the door of the closet to block herself, but she peeked around and could see Elysia holding court right down the hallway, with a cigarette in one hand and an early cocktail in the other. Sylvia leafed through the wallet, and, just for spite, lifted one hundred dollars out of it. She was instantly so enlivened that she went back into the group to prolong the experience, taken as if she were in a trance. Everything was heightened. The passage of time was different. Her mood was euphoric. She went around with a smile all day, treasuring her secret, like a bottle of juice in the barren desert. Nobody ever knew.

After the first time, she felt some guilt, but also so powerful and alert. She kept waiting for some repercussion, but it never happened. At first, she swore she would never do it again, but in her beating heart, Sylvia recognized that this was to be nothing less than her frenzy.

She loved going through their handbags, seeing all their intimate keepsakes - pills, condoms, sex toys, tampons, money, receipts, photographs. She saw hemorrhoid cream, laxatives and herpes medication and a miniature bottle of vodka, like they have on airplanes. She found three hundred dollars worth of black chips from the Commerce casino. Once, she discovered a snapshot of one consort nude on a beach with the husband of another; they all ran in the same clique. She liked prowling through their privacy, but she also got a thrill out of taking their stuff. Cash, of course, but anything which was stylish or could be of value was too tempting to resist. She took credit cards, gift cards, checkbooks, passports, driver's licenses, cell phones, watches, keychains, keys, lipstick, perfume, lighters, sunglasses, a roll of quarters, cigarettes, marijuana, medication. Her favorite was jewelry. She took a pair of pearl earrings and an antique broach. She stole a silver hip flask, a Mexican puzzle, an empty cylinder of Mace. She stole a sleek consumer flashlight that zapped a would-be assailant with an electric shock; she always kept the implement in her own purse after that. She stashed all the rest of her plunder, like trophies, in a cedar chest at the back of her walk-in closet.

Sylvia became absolutely brazen. She started to do it constantly, seeking out opportunities, and, of course, always trying to up the ante.

She soon became addicted to stealing from department stores.

She loved walking in through those polished glass doors, with all the neatly-presented merchandise gleaming and reflecting. The first thing that hit her as she strutted in was the scent of myriad perfumes, pressed garments, honeysuckle air, and the clean smell of everything new and immaculate. She loved all the display counters tended by attentive salespeople with luxurious offerings in fine jewelry, cosmetics, clothing, shoes and lingerie.

As if it had all been laid before her as a buffet of sumptuous consumables, she felt as if the full array of splendor was an invitation to her calculating wiles. If opportunity created the crime, then everything was an opportunity.

She always waited for her precise moment, after prowling around to see what pretty things caught her eye, and where there were flaws in the system that she could exploit. There were angles blocked from cameras, wares left unattended, distracted employees and unheeding customers.

Sylvia always dressed well in designer brands, with sophisticated make-up and her dark hair loose and flowing down her back, and she carried a few shopping packages to make the right impression. With packages, it looked as if she was already spending money, so she was well treated, and did not draw adverse attention. The shopping packages were mostly stuffed with paper to make them appear bulky, but that was how she often concealed her stolen items.

Nobody ever suspected her.

One day, she had a scare.

There was a uniformed security guard, Tyrell, handsome in a rough kind of a way, with a broken nose like a boxer, and a six o clock shadow. She had spotted him before, and she always checked for him before she ever made a move on anything.

She had been browsing in the lingerie department. When she found a silky green teddy with a snap crotch, she just dropped it from the rack into one of her shopping bags. She moved away at once, and pretended that something else had caught her eye at one of the other racks, but then she went over to the escalators and went down to the next level, which was perfume and fine jewelry, and then only steps away there was the exit to the clear street.

Ten yards from the door, she was glancing over the presentation at the fine jewelry counter, when, from behind her, she heard Tyrell's unmistakable deep voice,

"Excuse me. Can you come with me, please?"

She felt her bones grow cold, almost afraid to turn to face him. Reality had struck. This was the moment that she always dreaded. There was nothing worse than the guilty truth of being caught red-handed.

He was not talking to her.

He was talking to a teenage couple with a backpack, and he had his hands on his hips where his gun was hanging in his holster. He was dressed in a blue uniform with a silver badge on his chest and a pair of silver handcuffs in a pouch on his belt, and the way that he was standing made his muscles bulge.

"What's this about?" asked the teenage boy.

"I need to take a look in your backpack."

"Why? We haven't done anything," the girl protested.

"You were trying on shoes. I saw you take two new shoes out of the box, and gave the box back empty. Those shoes are in your backpack. Now, we can do this right here, or you can come with me."

Another security guard - a very tall redhead, with a badge and a nameplate that said Racquel - came walking up behind the couple.

The teenagers dropped their heads and shuffled along with the security personnel.

As he passed, Tyrell's eyes met Sylvia's. She was sure that he saw how flustered and ashamed she was, and that he knew everything about her.

That night, in the bathroom mirror, Sylvia stared at her reflection in the stolen lingerie. She felt so sexy the way the silky fabric embraced her curves. But, when she crawled into bed with her husband, Hector hardly noticed the new ensemble, and pushed her away as she tried to curl up beside him.

"Why are you such a grouch?" she pouted.

"Come on, Sylvia," he said, rolling onto his side with his back to her, "I had a long day. I'm flattened."

He was exhausted, that was true, because he was snoring within three minutes without even turning out the lights. Sylvia lay prone in bed, staring at the ceiling. As still as a lifeless body, she did not want to move, replaying the frozen moment when she expected to be arrested. It was impossible to sleep. She thought about how close she had come to getting caught. Sylvia had never been so unstrung in her life. She imagined the disgrace of the process, the way that those teenagers had been paraded in shame through the store, and she tried to imagine the dank, furtive hole where they were held. She could not believe that she had put herself in so much jeopardy, risking complete ruin, stigma and exposure in such a reckless way. It was utter folly. She did not know how she would have been able to break the news to Hector, bring in lawyers, endure the mockery of her circle and face the prospect of punishment.

She thought about Tyrell with his biceps bulging, and the way that he had looked at her.

As soon as morning broke, with hardly any sleep, she decided to race back to the department store.

She ate a hurried pastry for her breakfast. She drove her champagne-colored Lexus down Santa Monica Boulevard, which was thick with traffic in the morning heat. The sun climbed in the hot sky. She imagined Tyrell sweating in his uniform while he was coming in to work as she was headed to the same destination. Sylvia was not going to let him break her so effortlessly.

She had a plan.

There was a tennis bracelet - not the kind that would normally be out on display, but behind lock and key - that sat right there unprotected for the taking. It was a signature item for the department store, and on a special promotion. Encrusted with tiny diamonds, emeralds, opals, rubies and sapphires, it was presented open in its box on a raised stand on one of the countertops. Under the sparkle of its own miniature spotlight, a rainbow halo reflected off the colored gems. The attendant at the fine jewelry counter, an obese woman with thick wrists, who sat on a stool right behind the bracelet, was also responsible for its security. But, over the last weeks, Sylvia had been surveying the set-up, and she spotted a weakness. The woman got distracted sometimes, and, while her head was turned, Sylvia was convinced that she was adept enough to seize the bracelet.

It was at the end of an aisle so she would have to walk right up to it, picking her timing to perfection.

She watched from a slight distance, browsing through racks absently. The store was bustling with people; nobody wanted to leave the air-conditioning to go back out into the stifling heat. As people bunched about, it was easy for Sylvia to go unnoticed, and, using the racks as cover, she discreetly edged closer to her target. The bracelet drew her towards it like a beacon in a storm. As luck would have it, one of the other employees called the attendant over to another station for help with a register.

It was a perfect opening.

Sylvia strode down the aisle, heading straight for the gleam of the unguarded bracelet. Out of the corner of her eye, she saw that the woman was laughing with her co-worker, absorbed in their little moment of distraction.

She was upon it. Her heart was pounding. She let the mouth of her shopping bag gape open to receive the prize. It was at her fingertips. It would take one little flick and it would be hers. She almost took it, first with a quick look to the left and the right, and then she spotted Tyrell.

He was watching her from the other side, about twenty feet away.

She had not done anything yet. She was innocent. He could accuse her of nothing. She was just shopping. She did not touch the bracelet, and kept advancing towards him. He did not take his eyes off her, staring at her with a focus so penetrating it was as if he was looking through her clothing.

She could not help but to drop her gaze.

She brushed past him, and said, "Excuse me," in such a humble way that she immediately asked herself why she had felt it necessary to excuse herself, walking past him. It was a blunder. It made her seem guilty. She had nothing to apologize for.

He gave a little grunt of acknowledgement as she said it, as if he *did* excuse her. She hated herself for giving him that power without any resistance. Who was he to excuse her?

She kept walking, thinking that she could possibly circle back, and take another pass at the bracelet, that maybe the woman would take another break. But, when she glanced back to make sure that all was clear, Tyrell was still behind her. He was following her. He was not even trying to conceal the fact that he suspected her, and he was on her tail.

She tried to shake him off.

She weaved through the maze of counters and display cabinets in a random path, and used the mirrors to see if he was still trailing her. He did not follow in her footsteps, one by one, but he kept her in his sight, moving in the same direction.

She went up the escalator to the woman's clothing department. She did not dare to look back until she was halfway up, and there was only a boy with an ice cream, but, as she reached the top of the escalator, she saw Tyrell step onto the bottom.

Without hesitation, she snatched a dress from the rack, and went straight to the ladies' changing room, in an effort to disappear.

She drew the curtain. There was a bench, no more than a low shelf, and she sat down to catch her breath. She had evaded him. She could wait it out in there, until he figured he had lost the trail. Of course, there was no use in trying to get the bracelet now. He was onto her. She had to forget about it, no matter what. The main thing now, Sylvia thought, was just to slide out of there, and retreat into the ether. She wished she could vanish into nothing, that the floor would open and swallow her.

A saleswoman came past to ask if everything was okay in there, and Sylvia realized how long she had been sitting in the little booth. She was still not ready to put her head out.

"Uh-huh," she said, "Sorry, I had a phone call from the babysitter."

She should have known better, by going along with the pretence, but she had been shaken. It was important to act out the movements. She slipped out of her clothing and tried on the item she had picked. It was way too small, she had grabbed the wrong size in her hastiness. She let the dress drop to the floor, and as she looked down, following the natural descent of the clothing, she saw at the foot of the curtain of the dressing room - where the hem almost touched the carpet - Tyrell's boots.

Separated only by a flimsy curtain, in her bra and panties, she stood riveted, not knowing what to do.

He did not speak, but it was clear that he was listening, and she was sure that she could hear his breathing. His body heat seemed to permeate the fabric. In the shadow of the curtain was the shape of his silhouette. She wondered if he could hear the thump of her heart beating in dismay.

He stood vigil like a sentry, and it was the patient silence that was so unnerving to Sylvia. But, likewise, she stood immobile like a store mannequin in front of the mirror, petrified like prey in the scent of a predator, as he seemed to sniff the air.

She heard a grunt on the other side of the curtain, and then his boots disappeared, and, letting out a breath, she listened to him going away.

She did not know if it was a trap. Perhaps, he was just around the corner, waiting to pounce upon her. Sylvia tried to tell herself that she had no reason to worry because she had not removed the bracelet, and there was no evidence on her person. He could not detain her just for her thoughts. He could not detain her just for her guilt-ridden thoughts, even if there was some way that he could read them.

She could not keep hiding.

She got dressed again, and pulled back the curtain in one swift confident stroke. There were a few other customers waiting to use the dressing room. One woman rolled her eyes at Sylvia because she had been in there for so long. But, there was no sign of Tyrell.

Instead, there was Raquel.

The redhead made it clear that she was watching her. Raquel reached for her walkie-talkie, obviously calling for Tyrell who had gone scouring for her somewhere else. He would return at any second.

Sylvia had to keep moving.

She handed the garment to one of the store employees.

"Wrong size," she said, pointing out the label.

Sylvia headed for the exit, knowing that Raquel was trailing her, to make sure that she was off the premises.

A wave of heat hit her as she stepped into the sharp sunlight.

It was a narrow escape, but she had wriggled free. They clearly had their eyes on her from the beginning. They were alerted. This time, she promised herself that she would not go back, and, in fact, she recognized that it was impossible to go back. They had her picture. They had a file on her in their computer, which they would share throughout their network. They had that facial recognition software so that when she entered the store, there would be a red flag. She had to give up her pursuits now. It was too dangerous; if she continued, sooner or later, the odds were that she would get caught. She had to forget about the bracelet, no matter how much she craved having it in her collection.

Actually, most of the time, she did not even look at her collection of property unless she had the occasion to add something to it. On those occasions, she let her eyes wander lovingly across her souvenirs, remembering how each possession had come into her hands. The bracelet would have been a crowning glory.

Her life was a void again. She was back into the same coterie of tedious friends, and languishing through the long, listless days of the cruel summer. She yearned for some reason to be on fire. Other people found fulfillment. She wished she were a potter, an astronaut, a corporate woman climbing up the ladder, or the courtesan to a king. She wished that Hector Robles was a different kind of man, a man who would inspire her with passion, a man who could show passion toward her.

Of course, she could not stop thinking about Tyrell and the feral way he had hunted her through the department store. She thought about how their eyes had met, about the rugged contempt with which he had treated her. She remembered standing almost naked and defenseless, separated from him by only a thin curtain like a virgin behind a veil. She kept reliving the experience again and again in her mind. Terror or not, she felt drawn to the emotion. She hated having to deny herself. She had escaped, and she had no reason to believe she was in any kind of trouble, but she knew that it was fatal to go back there.

About ten days after the incident, nostalgic already for the path she had abandoned, Sylvia felt an urge to examine her cedar chest of treasures. She could not resist her impulses even though she was aware that she might feel tempted to seek more plunder to add to the coffers. The chest was under a cloth, behind some hanging clothes at the back of her closet. She unlocked it, and began to wade through the different items, one by one.

She played with a string of pearls, which she had taken from the department store. She fondled a single earring. She flicked a lighter which she had stolen from Elysia right off the table, and she remembered how gratifying it was to watch her search for it afterwards with an unlit cigarette dangling from her mouth. She picked up Elysia's driver's license and her comb, with a wisp of her blonde hair. She wished she knew how to do voodoo so that she could pierce a needle through her effigy. She could not believe how much she had stolen from Elysia, and she was gripped by a cold rage as she imagined how she would feel if Elysia ever stole anything from her.

Her collection of stolen property was an absolute secret, and Sylvia wondered if perhaps Hector had an absolute secret too, and his own chest of skeletons in the back of his closet.

She had searched through so many private purses, rifled through contraband, and explored the hidden foibles of others, but she had not ever conducted that kind of scrutiny on her own husband.

It was the middle of the morning. Hector was at the bank.

When she started to peel through his things, rummaging around the racks and drawers of his dressing room, it did not take long to discover what her husband was hiding. A jacket that smelled of familiar smoke. A smudge of recognizable lipstick on a shirt thrown into the dry cleaning hamper. A love note to Hector with Elysia's signature.

He could not bring himself to destroy the documentation.

What enraged Sylvia was that the breach had been right under her nose. She did not care about his infidelity; that was a trifle. She was not grief-stricken about his extra-marital adventuring, she found it pathetic. She was furious that she had been deceived. There was nothing worse to a thief than to be tricked. The point of the malfeasance was to outwit the victim. She hated being a victim to the two of them. She felt like a fool.

Sylvia bolted the front door.

When Hector came home that evening, Sylvia would not let him into the house.

"Come on, Sylvia," he said to her through the front door, "Let me in. What's going on?"

It was a heavy door, with beveled glass panes, where they could make out the blur of one another on opposite sides.

"I know what's going on, Hector," she said to him, without unlocking the door.

"What are you talking about? Open up."

"You are having an affair with Elysia."

He paused to take it in before he responded. "Wherever would you get an idea like that?"

"You took her to Cancun, Hector, when you were supposed to be in Dallas on business. She wrote a letter thanking you for the trip. It meant so much to you that you kept the letter."

"Let's talk inside."

"I don't want you in the house," Sylvia concluded, "Go away."

He stood out there for a while, ringing the bell, pounding and shouting, but then she turned out all the lights, and he got back into his BMW in the darkness, and took off down the driveway. She did not try to guess where he was going because she did not care, but, in some way, it was the last straw.

She could not stand it any longer. She felt that she was going to explode. That night, she was alone in bed, with an empty hollow where Hector usually slept. He was not on her mind. What was gnawing at her consciousness was the bracelet. Compared to the impression made by her husband, the idea of the bracelet could fill an abyss. It was almost like a mystical amulet granting invincibility. The possession of the bracelet seemed to be the only thing in the world that mattered.

She tossed and turned all night, picturing the colored blocks of the gemstones, emitting a myriad of radiant hues. It was never about the money, and now it was not even about the thrill of the theft. For Sylvia, the craving was beyond feverish. It was like a conquest which she had to achieve for her own survival.

The next morning was another sweltering day. Tempers were short. Traffic was at a standstill on the way to the department store. Sylvia had ample time to regain her composure, to calm down, to change her actions. It was her prerogative to change her mind, sometimes, even at the last second if she sensed danger. But, instead of turning around, she was frantic. Stuck in a morass of traffic, she slammed her palms on the steering wheel in frustration. Off the boulevard, she tried to find a different route, turning into a sidestreet to find herself stuck behind a car that overheated.

It was as if the universe were plotting against her, she thought, but it could have been an omen.

She kept to her lucky patterns. As usual, she chose to park in the outdoor lot; she did not want to get trapped underground while trying to make a getaway. As she walked across the lot in her red-soled shoes, the glare of the sunlight on the parking lot surface radiated heat from below, like the flames of hell. It was such a relief when she finally swept through the gleaming glass doors, and the cool succor of the air-conditioning.

She went into her character, and marched down the aisle. Her plan was to make a lightning strike, before anyone even knew that she was in the store. There would be no taking her time to get a lay of the land. She was not going to do anything other than the lightest reconnaissance, but walk right up to the bracelet without hesitation, seize it and get straight out again.

Sure enough, as she approached, the attendant was nowhere in sight, and with a quick look to the left and right, Sylvia saw that she was safe. It was now or never. As if she were in a dream she approached it, lifted the jewels from the display, and dropped the prize into her purse. She had it. It worked.

She headed directly for the exit.

But, as if appearing from nowhere, Tyrell blocked her path. "You're going to have to come with me."

"I haven't done anything."

"Then you won't have anything to worry about. But you're going to have to come with me."

Sylvia saw how he looked over her shoulder, and she glanced back, and Racquel was walking up behind her. They had been ready for her. It was a trap, and she had swallowed the bait.

"You know how much money I spend in this place?" Sylvia demanded. "Suppose I say no?"

"Cuff her," Tyrell instructed.

"Yep," responded Racquel, and before Sylvia knew it, there was a metallic clack, and the security guard had her wrists handcuffed behind her back.

People in the store stopped to stare, and Sylvia felt a flush run through her entire body.

"Now, you'll come," Tyrell said, taking her by the upper arm, and leading her towards a service stairwell.

Racquel took hold of her on the other side to help her down the stairs in her heels.

It was a short flight - with one step missing - which took them to a restricted area behind double doors covered in canvas. Without speaking, they walked down the concrete surface of a bleak hallway, with no aperture to air or light but a lurid pink glow from no apparent source. It was such a foul atmosphere that Sylvia could hardly breath. In custody, it was as if she was being led away from the world, and that nobody would ever know what became of her. She imagined the two teenagers following this route, and realized that whatever had happened to them was about to happen to her.

She was taken into an office where there was a desk and a table, but no chairs and no windows. There was a white board with measurements to show height from five feet to six feet. The room had a stale smell of body odor and flat air.

Raquel put Sylvia's things onto the table.

Without hesitation, Tyrell snapped open her purse, plunged his hand inside and retrieved the bracelet.

"This is what we call hard evidence," he pronounced, dangling the glittering bracelet from his fingers, "You have been caught shoplifting."

Racquel said, "We got you."

He withdrew her driver's license from her purse. He glanced at it, and then at Racquel and announced, "Sylvia Robles. Beverly Hills."

"Filthy criminal," said Racquel.

To Sylvia, it was obvious how much they were both relishing their dominion. This was one of the perks of their employment. She was sure that this was how they treated everyone who came down that ominous tunnel. They each had a little smirk, and a sarcastic tone, and the swagger of control. They were well practiced, like they were running some kind of racket of their own.

"I want you to know something," he said, coming up to her, "You could be in very deep trouble here. In some ways, that's up to you. I want you to know something else that's very important. We have not called the police..."

"Not yet," added Racquel, folding her arms.

"Please, don't..."

"If you cooperate, we might not have to call the police, so in that way, it's up to you," advised Tyrell.

"I'm cooperating," Sylvia said, without looking him in the eye.

"Good," he praised, then he said to Racquel, "I'm going to run her ID."

"Okay, I'll finish up the search," Racquel said.

Tyrell said, "You are going to be searched thoroughly for weapons as well as stolen property." He walked behind her, touching the handcuffs. "The female officer will conduct the search." He unlocked the cuffs, and let her hands free. "I suggest you comply."

"I need you to undress," Racquel instructed, as Tyrell walked out of the office.

Sylvia stepped out of her clothes, rubbing her wrists where she had been manacled. She watched Racquel open a drawer on the desk, and extract a set of rubber gloves. The security guard pulled them on finger by finger, with a snap as the rubber fell into place.

"Oh yes, honey," Racquel smiled wickedly, "We need to make sure that there's nothing else. And you would be surprised at where people try to hide all sorts of things."

"There's nothing else," said Sylvia, "I promise."

"Let's make sure," Racquel said, dumping all the contents of Sylvia's purse onto the table.

Wearing the rubber gloves, she began raking through the contents, and came upon the taser that Sylvia always carried around, since she had stolen it at a nightclub.

"What the hell is this?" Racquel reacted, "A weapon!"

Before Sylvia could say a word, Racquel walked right out of the room with the taser, and slammed the door.

Sylvia was left alone, stripped, defenseless. Even in that oppressive room, every pore on her body tingled. She felt sticky all over. She had the same feeling as when she was in the dressing room, and Tyrell was on the other side of the sheer fabric. She wanted to scream but she was too afraid to move.

The door burst open, and Tyrell stormed in, with Racquel behind him, still wearing the rubber gloves.

"A weapon!" he exploded, coming right up to her face with no discretion to the fact that she was in a state of undress, "Do you know how much trouble you are in now?" He held up the taser. "That makes this a possible violent robbery. You could be charged with assault. You could end up in prison."

Standing naked, with her hands at her sides as he loomed over her in his sweaty uniform, she seemed to be watching the scene from outside herself. Nobody knew where she was in this poky office under the authority of strangers, a subject of their whims. She felt so aroused in manifold ways, as he relished her vulnerable exposure. He treated her as if she was not only beneath courtesy and dignity, but beneath his footing. He exuded arrogance and superiority. He leered at her as if she was a pet or a plaything to him.

Tyrell clicked the switch of the taser and an ominous buzz crackled to life.

"How would you feel..." he began, the sides of his lips curling in a smile, "...if someone used this on you?"

She gasped, anticipating his intentions.

"It's on the mildest setting," he taunted, "See how you like it."

He touched the spark of the device to the tip of her exposed nipple. The shock was pain and pleasure all at once to her. She let her head fall back, moaning. He ran the spark up and down along her body, which felt like a prickle of needles jabbing into her flesh, and then to the other breast, and applied the spark to her other nipple. The intensity of the entire sensation was overwhelming, and, in the stuffiness of the room, jolted by electricity, Sylvia was sure that she was going to faint.

"What do you think?" Tyrell said, not to Sylvia, but to Racquel.

"I think she learnt something. I think she's had enough for today."

"Yes..." she pleaded, "I've had enough. I promise. I will be good."

"So, we're not going to call the cops on you, even though we could. But, just remember, Mrs Sylvia Robles, we know everything about you now. We know where you live. We have your address in Beverly Hills. We have evidence that you stole. We'll be in touch."

Tyrell walked out of the room.

"You can get dressed and go," Racquel said, in a contemptuous way, as she followed him, pulling the door closed.

Sylvia rocked back and forth on her feet, and put out a hand to steady herself. She felt a shudder go down her spine - of relief, of emotion, of intensity - and had to take several deep breaths to settle. She was trembling as she got dressed and bundled together her things, desperate to leave the confines of the claustrophobic office. As she reached for the door handle, it occurred to her that they might have left her locked in; the handle stuck at first, but then it turned, and she found herself in the desolate hallway without ventilation. She did not know where she was, but there was a gloomy pink exit sign at the far end, so she headed towards it, her legs shaking.

In the parking lot, she sat in her car, not able to drive, not even sure where she wanted to go. Home was not inviting. Sylvia just wanted to rest in the comfortable leather seats of her Lexus, as if she could remain there till the end of her days

She kept thinking about his parting words that he would be in touch. She could not imagine what there would be to be in touch about. It could have been a casual joke. He had said it so glibly that he might have been bluffing, but he seemed so sure of himself. It was clear that he was in cahoots with the smirking redhead. Sylvia wondered how many other culprits had been strip-searched. This was not the first time they had shaken someone down. They had a scheme. Things were destined to unravel. Sylvia worried that they would try to blackmail her. She was ripe for exploitation. She tried to anticipate what kind of demands they might make, how she might satisfy them. She feared that - after they had finished toying with her - they would expose her.

She was not paying attention to the time, but, as she sat there, fixated on Tyrell, she was amazed to see him emerge from the building in his uniform, and saunter across the parking lot. She saw his handcuffs and his holster. It was if she had manifested his appearance through the intensity of her focus. She was filled with panic, and was about to speed away, but then she realized that he had not come for her, and he was unaware that she was watching him.

His shift was over. He was heading for his car.

On the spot, she decided to take advantage of the opportunity. She realized that he had often been watching her without her knowledge; now the tables were turned. She started the Lexus.

He was driving a dented Ford sedan, and he headed down Santa Monica Boulevard towards the 405 Freeway North. In the congested traffic, it was easy to remain unseen, and because the cars were crawling so slowly, it was easy for her to keep him in sight. He had his guard down because he had no reason to assume he was being followed. Once they got onto the freeway, it was still bumper to bumper, so it was not difficult to follow him into the valley to North Hollywood.

Sylvia tracked Tyrell all the way to his home. The neighborhood was disgusting; there was nothing but fast-food restaurants, gas stations, tire shops and convenience stores. In the summer heat, a layer of smog hung over the city, and a haze steamed off the asphalt.

Tyrell lived in one of those nondescript two-story apartment buildings where the car was parked beneath the residence. She drove past the building as he turned into his parking space, and made a U-turn a little further along the block to come back just in time to see him going through the mesh security gate into the open courtyard.

As soon as he was out of sight, Sylvia parked her car along the street.

His name was on the list of residents at the front door, which also listed his apartment number.

If he knew where she lived, then now Sylvia knew where he lived too.

She did not know what she was going to do with that information, but knowledge is power. She did not have a strategy, she was improvising. She always wanted to see where this would go. She was in this position - being arrested - because she wanted to see where things would go. She always longed for the secrets of what happened behind the scenes, how the magic trick was done, the glamour of illusion. There was a luster in having the shrewdness of a thief, the confidence of a thief, the daring of a thief.

She waited, pretending to look for her key, and as soon as someone came out through the gate, Sylvia got hold of it before it closed, and walked in with a polite smile and a thank you.

A kidney-shaped swimming pool took up most of the courtyard. Two men, in wet swimwear, sat dangling their hairy legs into the water. A sign cautioned that there was no lifeguard on duty, and no diving was permitted.

There were two stairwells leading up to the second story, which was open to the pool on the one side. Sylvia went up the first set of stairs towards Tyrell's apartment number.

There was a smell of burnt chicken, and cat urine, and Sylvia noticed that each unit seemed to have the television volume turned up loud but never on the same channel.

Beside each front door, there was a living room window that looked out onto the pool. Some of the windows had blinds, but some allowed for a clear view in or out, so if she could see into his apartment, there was a chance that he could see her. Open to view, in one room was a big-bellied man in his boxers, and, in another, a woman nursing a baby. If she did not turn back, Sylvia would have to take the risk and cross in front of Tyrell's window, not knowing if it would be covered with blinds, not knowing if he might be looking out at the moment that she crossed.

Sylvia did not turn back, but as she came up to his front door, she was relieved when she saw that there were blinds on his window, and she would be able to cross unseen. She listened for a moment outside, hearing his television set turned to a ball game.

She imagined him on the other side, just behind the blinds, sitting in a T-shirt and flannels, a beer in his hand, maybe a can of nuts. She wondered what it would be like to live in that space. To her, it was like a cell, and if she lived there, she would be his prisoner and he would be her jailer. She saw his shower-bathtub, with a grimy rim, and a sodden wooden mat, and a toothbrush in a stained jar on the sink. She pictured the contents of his refrigerator - sixpack, salsa, a carton of milk, some salami - and his bedroom, with a bed that filled most of the room, and a dresser with a mirror taking up the rest.

It was so belittling that such a coarse man wielded such power and disdain.

She decided to knock on the door and confront him. She would demand his apology. She would threaten to report him to his employer. She would let him know that she knew his secrets too, that she had found the way to where he lived and slept. She would insinuate lawsuits, harassment, bodily assault from hired enforcers. She wondered what he would do when he opened the door and recognized her.

Sylvia was startled by a splash from the pool, where the two men had dipped into the water to cool off. She snapped out of her reverie, and realized that she was not thinking like a thief. She needed a more artful play than a direct conflict. Instead of a showdown, slinking by unseen, she scooted down the far stairwell and back to her car.

There had been enough excitement for one day, she told herself, as she pulled away into the snarl of traffic.

About six blocks from his apartment, there was a motel with a neon sign which was flashing uselessly during the brightness of the summer day. She drove through an archway to enter the parking lot, ringed by a dozen rental bungalows and one hutch with a printed sign, reading OFFICE. The man across the counter flap was young and insolent, with a face full of pimples, and when Sylvia asked if she could see one of the rooms, he told her she was welcome to inspect the room after she left a twenty dollar key deposit. She gave him the twenty, and then he let her have the key for ten minutes to look over the premises.

The room itself was exactly as she imagined. There were two twin beds pushed together, beneath a single paper-thin bedspread of faded yellow. The bedside pedestals bore circular stains of cups and bottles, and brownish streaks where lit cigarettes had been left burning. There was a carpet with what appeared to be semen residue. The walls were painted in a lime color, which had peeled in one corner near the ceiling, and on one wall was a picture of a mountain landscape in a plastic frame. The windows looked as if they had not been opened in months. The summer heat trapped a musty scent in the stuffy room.

She turned on the air conditioning, and, with a wheeze, it came to life, blowing cool air on her face.

After her long drive across town, she had to use the toilet in the adjoining bathroom. There was only a square of toilet paper on the roll, and an odd smell from the drains. When she flushed, the liquid rose tantalizingly to the top of the toilet bowl, as if it was about to spill over onto the mat, but slowly oozed into the sewer through whatever was blocking the flow. There was a hiss from the plumbing as the tank filled up again.

She went back to the office, and she gave the clerk another three hundred dollars in cash to keep the room for the rest of the week, then she got back into her Lexus and headed out of the valley and through the leafy canyons to her home in Beverly Hills.

When she drove through the automatic gates, she saw her husband's BMW parked in his spot in the driveway.

Hector had got into the house.

There was a trail of rose petals on the front doorstep, and he was waiting for her in the lobby, with a bouquet of red roses.

"I am here to apologize," her husband announced, dropping to one knee with the roses cradled in his arms, "I broke it off with Elysia. I want to come home."

"I want a divorce, Hector," said Sylvia.

"I had a huge fight with her," he confessed, "It's over. Please, Sylvia, let me have a second chance."

"It's too late, anyway," Sylvia declared, "I've fallen in love with someone else."

She went upstairs and packed a bag, including a roll of toilet paper, which is what she had intended to do in any case, but it also helped avoid the brewing altercation about where Hector was going to spend the night. Of course, he wanted to stay in the house, and was likely to stamp his foot down. She did not really care where he stayed now, because she was leaving.

She drove straight back to North Hollywood to Tyrell's apartment.

Once again, it was easy to get into the courtyard, and, slip unnoticed up the steps to his unit. She listened with her ear pressed to his front door. There was not a sound. It seemed that he was not home. She imagined where he might be - working out at the gym, having a sundowner in some local joint, or back on a late shift at work.

Even with the inviting swimming pool, the courtyard below was too hot to occupy. Nobody was about. The scorching summer had left the hillsides dry as tinder, and far-off fires spread a creeping pallor of smoke across the valley.

She had to recognize that her own cravings had led her to this point.

Sometimes, she wondered if she had lost her mind, she was so frantic, she just kept going and going like a fanatic. But perhaps that was not obsession but passion; perhaps that lunacy was simply what it meant to be a human being; perhaps it was vital to being alive. She did not think it would be a better life to exist with nothing inside; it was better to be just crazy enough. If we were all freaks, we were none of us freaks.

It was not for her to pronounce the judgement whether Tyrell was to live or die for his actions, but she did not want to be his captive, and, if it was necessary for him to die for her to protect herself, she decided that she would kill him. It seemed like the logical progression of her lawless path. She thought about how easy it would be to do it. She would wield her skills to trick him. She would lure him under false pretences. The crime comprised motive, opportunity and means. She had motive, she needed to concoct the opportunity, and she would engineer it so that her victim would bring her the means. She would use his own handcuffs to restrain him, and his own gun as the murder weapon.

She left a note on his door for him to come and find her.

As night fell, a lurid glow from the neon sign, pulsing above the archway entrance to the motel, illuminated Sylvia's room. A lone bedside lamp on the sullied pedestal offered a flicker of warm light. A scent of perfume lingered in the air - she had sprayed a few spurts in an effort to create an ambiance. The trickling water from the bathroom gurgled like a mountain stream. Outside, the occasional siren punctuated the steady rumble of the nocturnal traffic; inside, slow music was playing. She had brought her own fluffy pillows from home, and she stretched out invitingly on the bed.

She waited, thinking of nothing but her plot. Her mind could not entertain another thought. She imagined how it would play out. She would entice him, and make sure his defenses were lowered, then try to get the handcuffs on him, try to get hold of his gun. She would make a game out of it. She would keep it playful and titillating. She would have to find the right moment, understanding that it might take time to get him into a vulnerable situation. It was crucial not to hesitate in that split-second gap to pull the trigger.

She had not given too much thought to the aftermath because the hardest part was the execution. She was not going to deal with disposing of a body, or coming up with an elaborate ruse. She would see what the possibilities for alibis were when the deed was accomplished. She was not concerned because there were so many ways that she could stage it: as a suicide, as a sex accident, as some kind of self-defense story, if it was even necessary. What she was hoping was that after the gunshot she would have enough time to get the hell out of there and vanish. There would be nothing to connect the two of them, after he was gone. She would be able to move on, and, once she had this down, for certain, her next quarry was going to be Elysia.

She did not feel impatient, because she knew how this was going to end, and laying in wait was a necessary component of the crime, but she could hardly contain her anticipation. She kept checking her appearance in the mirror, adjusting her cleavage, listening at the door, peering through the dusty windows which would not open. She had to be ready at any moment.

Around nine p.m., there was a knock at the door of the motel room.

"It's open," Sylvia called from the bed, where she struck a seductive pose in her sheer teddy with the crotch snap.

The handle turned and, at first the door did not open, as if the person on the other side was expecting a booby trap. Slowly, it inched open, crack by crack, and, without showing his face, he held out his hand with her note between his fingers. She could see the cuff of his uniform.

"I got your note," Tyrell said, "On my front door."

"Come in," she said.

He stepped into the room, pulling the door shut behind him. He looked around the squalid place, and took it all in, including the sultry way she was lying on the bed. "Mind telling me what's going on?"

"Like I wrote in the note, you said you were going to be in touch. I never heard from you. So I tracked you down. I needed to talk to you."

"What do you want?" he asked, not sounding so guarded now, as his blind ego started to do the work for her.

"I want to confess," she said, in a husky voice, "Come over here."

"You look very fashionable," he commented, edging closer.

"Well, that's one of the things I wanted to confess to you. I stole this lingerie from your store."

He laughed. "Yep, that does look like one of ours."

She patted the bed, and, adjusting his holster, he sat down beside her. She told herself to get him at ease, and then - like any lawbreaker - wait until a prospect presented itself before she made her move.

"Are you going to punish me?" she teased.

"What else did you want to confess?" he asked.

She said it in a very coy way. "That when you searched me...with the other guard..."

"Racquel. My associate. Yes, she's strict."

"She's a very striking woman. I know you were doing your job and I was in trouble but it was very alluring to me."

"Go on," he instructed, "Be specific."

A siren wailed outside, and then the street grew quiet, and all they could hear was the slow music in the motel boudoir.

"That thing you did to me with the electricity..." she said, as if each word was a shock to her tongue.

"Yes...you liked that?"

"Yes," she breathed, "I loved that. I have to admit it." She came in close to him now, and they kissed. She had meant it to be part of the act, but Sylvia had to acknowledge how satisfying it was to have a man kiss her like that, and feeling his strong body against her. She had to pull away from him to keep going with the plan.

"So," she said, purring into his ear, "I was thinking...your handcuffs..."

He laughed, reaching for his pouch. "So, you want me to put the handcuffs on you again?"

"Or maybe this time, you should wear the handcuffs."

She would not have to kill him, if she could keep kissing him forever.

The Blindfold

A few flakes of frost descended in the dark night, and only the glow of lights from the restaurant illuminated the parking lot, where Ken was waiting for Monica. They had never met, so she told him that, since they were going out for sushi, she could be identified by her Japanese dress which looked like a kimono. As he watched her strut up to the restaurant, with the square cut of black hair framing her face, and her wicked smile, adding to the impact, it was clear that she was wearing a wig.

Ken and Monica had been introduced by a mutual friend, who thought they might have a few things in common. The friend was surprised that the two of them did not already know each other, since they all moved in the same circle.

The restaurant was an L-shaped place, dimly-lit in the glimmer of Japanese lanterns. There were thin rice paper partitions between the tables, so they sat at a booth at the back, to be able to talk candidly, because they both knew that, sooner or later, the conversation would roll around to their kinky tastes.

"What I like," she confided, after the octopus sashimi had been served, "Is not so much a feeling of submission as of powerlessness. I'm tough, ninety nine per cent of the time. I'm an artist, but I am also in the corporate world. I have to make a hundred decisions a day."

"You walked in like a boss," Ken nodded, admiring her under the soft lighting.

"So, sometimes, I just want to let go, and not to be me. I just want to close my eyes, and not know who is there. Nameless. Disguised."

"Like wearing a wig."

Monica gave him a sexy smirk. "You'll find out."

"I saw this scene once," he shared, leaning in across the square table, "At a fetish club, past downtown where it gets industrial. Like what you are describing. A man led a woman on a chain through the crowd. She was dressed in leather from her corset to her tall boots. Her breasts exposed. Around her neck was a leather collar. Her eyes were completely covered with a blindfold..."

"What kind of blindfold?" Monica asked.

"It was very particular," he remembered, "Because, it was in leather like all the rest, but there were eyes painted on the outside of the leather."

"Eyes?"

"Yes, they looked as real as fear. There was an expression in the painted eyes that was enticing."

"What kind of expression?" she asked, looking at him over the rim of her *sake* cup.

"Wide-eyed.   Vulnerable.   Maybe arousal."

Monica put her cup down on the table. "But the woman could not see...?"

"No, not a thing." Ken refilled her drink, and poured another for himself. "Her partner was a sort of typical dominant, with a shaved head, and goatee. Muscles bulging through his cut off leather vest. Might have had a tattoo. He was gentle and protective, and she had those wobbly boots, although they looked great on her legs, so he had to be responsible for her safety..."

"How do you like the octopus?" she asked, pointing with her chopstick.

"Delicious."

There was a lemony trace to it, leaving the faintest scent. The candles flickered in the lanterns. The mutter of conversation from the other diners was low.

The couple at the next booth stood up to leave, and Ken waited until they walked away before he continued.

"So, he takes her into the dungeon of the club, and ties her up, spread out in a strange chair...almost like a gynecologist's chair, but stylish...and then, men and women are wandering in, and fondling her, and she spends the night writhing in ecstasy without ever knowing who touched her."

Monica put down her chopsticks. "Did you touch her?"

"Yes," Ken acknowledged, "Almost everyone did. All over her body. There were different instruments available - a pinwheel, a feather, an electric wand. It was all about the anonymous sensations."

"I have never seen anything like that."

"I hope I didn't shock you. Arwyn said that you had a wild side..."

"Oh, I do...I'm hardly shocked."

"Well, tell me something about you that I would not have suspected."

"Right now, in my purse, I have a certain fetish item. I am not saying what it is. I will allow you to imagine. But I carry it around as a reminder. To keep me balanced."

They stopped because the waitress brought the next course, a rainbow roll, and another flask of *sake*, and then, they let the conversation drift away from the kink, knowing that they had broken the ice, knowing that they would come back to it, just teasing each other along with the occasional hidden meaning in the conversation, and subtle glances between them.

They were the last table to leave, and Ken walked Monica to her car. He slid into the passenger seat, because it was cold out now, and they both wanted to keep talking.

The windows of the car misted up, as if a white veil had fallen over them.

"So," she said, coming all the way back to the topic now that it was just the two of them in private, "Did you guess the item I am carrying?"

"It has to be able to fit in your purse. A gag, maybe."

"No," she said, lowering her eyes.

"Handcuffs?"

"That would also be a no."

The passing headlights were a misty blur through the translucent windshield.

"Don't tell me that it's a blindfold?"

She opened her purse, and showed him the leather blindfold. There were two captivating eyes painted onto the front.

"Like the woman in the club," he recognized.

The lights from the restaurant darkened, and the shroud of mist turned to black.

"Was there anything else that was striking about her?" she asked.

"Yes." Ken's face lit up, as Monica started the car. "Her hair was purple."

The Disciple

(for Lara)

Pandora came in at the last minute, as a replacement for one of the other performers. The first time they met was in her dressing room, and Roark spent a half hour getting to know her, which was far too long when he was needed on the set, and the assistant director had to come looking for him. She photographed well, and exuded a magnetic presence on screen, and she was so easy to work with that he did not understand why she had a reputation for being difficult, in fact, psychotic.

He should have seen the clues in her eyes, which were hazel and limpid, but which flashed with a fiery glow that he had only ever seen once before in a cinematographer who was ultimately committed to an asylum. She was tall with straight, dirty blonde hair and a sinewy tanned body, with apple-sized breasts and a famous round rump.

After the movie wrapped, he did not give her another thought until he ran into her months later at the Cannes Film Festival in the south of France. They were at a press dinner, and he went over to her table, picking up the conversation where they had left off in the dressing room on the North Hollywood sound stage when she was doing his movie. She was dressed in a shimmering evening gown, and he was in a tuxedo, and they sat at a round ten-person table with an elaborate floral centerpiece and white tablecloth, flecked with breadcrumbs. He was planning to shoot something else in Cannes - he had brought a star in tow with him from Los Angeles - but he thought that there might be a role in it for Pandora too. He was staying at a villa in the hills with the French producer named Philippe, among a group of international houseguests who were there for the festival or the production. Roark was the only one of the Americans who could speak French, and Philippe was the only Frenchman who could speak English, and so, with no other common languages, the two of them had to translate for everyone else in the group. Pandora came to stay there after a few days, while they were making the movie, but they all had their own rooms, and the star who had come with him from Los Angeles did not like the way that Pandora behaved around him, making eyes, and sharing private jokes. They sat side-by-side at every meal, and sometimes picked the *hors d'oeuvres* off one another's plate.

The production and the festival came to an end, and everyone who was staying in the house began peeling off one by one to different destinations. Some returned to L.A., some journeyed on to other European locations. One morning, when Philippe was shuttling the last of the guests along the coastal freeway to the airport in Nice, Roark and Pandora were left alone in the villa for the first time.

He locked the front door from the inside, so that they would not be accidentally disturbed.

He could not find her. He checked her room - the door was wide open - then he went downstairs, out to the swimming pool, but she was not anywhere to be found, almost as if she was hiding. He called out for her, but she did not respond, like they were playing some sort of cat-and-mouse game. He went back into the house, and from the far end of the hallway, he saw her coming out of a spare bedroom, barefoot on the hardwood floors, wearing nothing but cut-off shorts and a pink tank top. She caught sight of him, and there was a flicker of fear in her eyes, and she darted back into her own room, and tried to close the door.

In a few strides, he ran down the corridor before she could get the door shut, and he pushed it open, and she was right in front of him, afraid to move. Before they knew what they were doing, he slapped her across the face. The sting of his palm was like an electric shock.

"We're finally alone," he taunted, "There's nobody in the house to save you."

All of their flirting and innuendoes had led up to this. She fell back onto the bed, and he got on top of her. He groped her and fondled her, holding her down by clutching a handful of her hair. She fought back. She tried to kick him and knee him in the groin, so he smothered her with his weight and strength. She bit into his shoulder - so hard that there were teeth marks - and he got his forearm across her mouth. She tried to scratch him with her long polished fingernails, so he grabbed hold of her wrists and pinned her like a child having a tantrum until she stopped struggling. They lay like that face to face, fully clothed, breathing heavily, grinding together, feeling the heat of one another's bodies.

Then they heard the front door open, and Philippe was back from the airport, with his keys in his hand.

"Why is everything locked?" Philippe asked.

They came out of her room, and Philippe could tell that he had interrupted something, like the witness to a crime in progress. They all went out to the pool, and lay on the *chaises-longues*. Speaking in French, Philippe reminded Roark about his wife in Los Angeles.

Pandora caught the gist of it, and asked, "So you're married?"

"Yes."   Roark looked into her glimmering eyes. "I want to be clear about that."

"I am supposed to go to Italy tomorrow," she said.

"I am going to Paris," he told her, "Why don't you come to Paris with me?"

Before she even had a chance to respond, Philippe said, "If you have never been to Paris, you have to go to Paris."

On their last night in Cannes, they slept in separate rooms, on different floors of the villa, but, as he lay in bed, Roark thought about what he had done to her in the afternoon and what he was going to do to her when they got to Paris the next day. It was all about to unfold.

Philippe drove them to the airport in Nice, and they said their good-byes. Roark and Pandora checked in for the flight, and, as they went towards the gate, he reached down, and, for the first time, they linked hands, twisting their fingers together.

In Paris, they stayed at a three-star hotel in Montparnasse, above a bistro and a bakery. They were on the second floor up a spiral staircase. The room was spacious by Parisian standards, at an odd L-shape, dark with faded lime wallpaper and heavy furniture under a musty smell. There was an armoire on ball-and-claw legs, a bulky chest of drawers made of dark wood, and a solid bed with a soft mattress. Through the lace curtains of the French windows, standing at the black, metal grillwork, they could see down to the terrace of the bistro, decked with umbrellas branded with the advertising logos of popular *aperitifs*, and, beyond, across the gray roofs and chimney pots of Paris.

That night, he stripped her naked and posed her on all fours on top of the chest of drawers. Her long hair hung down, her eyes were blindfolded with her own scarf. She moaned and whimpered as he teased her for hours, exploring every pore of her body. Pandora did not travel without her own crop, and he used it on her gently at first, but she wanted it harder and harder. He never had the *sang-froid* to crop her as hard as she desired, no matter how she begged for it. It was not enough for her if there weren't welts and bruises painted across her buttocks. She wanted to be marked, for the pure adrenaline rush of it, and so that she could savor the experience afterwards, and maintain a sense of submission to him.

In the morning, with the sun streaming across the Parisian rooftops, they lay in bed together as if they had known one another since they were teenage sweethearts. The smell of freshly-baked baguettes rose from the bakery. The lace curtains fluttered in the window-frame. Together in their room, it seemed like there was nobody else in the entire world, as if the planet had ceased turning on its axis, and come to a sudden halt.

They rode the Metro from Montparnasse rattling along the grimy underground tunnels to the opulence of the Champs-Elysees, and before they came up the escalator from the station to the street, he covered her eyes with his hands. He led her out to the traffic island in the center of the grand Avenue, in the midst of all the squeaky horns and clatter, and pointed her so that when he took his hands away, she was staring up at the Arc de Triomphe.

"Now, whenever you see a picture of this monument, in a movie or a magazine, you will always think of me," he said.

As the sun fell, they had a leisurely dinner at a quiet restaurant on the left bank. They sat outside in the languor of the evening, and ate oysters and *torteau* on a bed of crushed ice, with a bottle of Muscadet. A boy came by with a basket of roses for sale, and he bought Pandora a single stem. After dinner, they strolled along the Seine, past the looming gothic cathedral of Notre-Dame, and watched the *bateaux-mouches* chugging down the river and beneath the old bridges. Lights from the boats and from the banks reflected on the ripples. Under the streetlamps, with a spring breeze drifting through her hair, she looked so young and beautiful that he could not believe that she was on his arm.

"I hope she costs you a fortune," a passer-by yelled at him in French.

Roark translated for Pandora, and they all laughed about it.

On the way back to where they were staying, they found themselves alone in a cobblestone street. He ordered her to get on her knees on the dirty stones, and kiss his boots. Instantly acquiescent, she dropped, leaving an imprint of her fresh red lipstick pressed in supplication against the leather toe of his boot, like the crimson rose resting on the sullen ground. He cupped the heel of his other boot on the back of her neck, keeping her in place. They did not move from the provocative tableau, understanding that the longer they remained in position, the more risk there would be of being discovered. Nobody came, and he gently raised her to his lips, and they kissed - closed mouthed - like a father and child, rather than lovers.

Back in the little world of their little room, he tied her wrists to the metal grillwork at the window with one of his silk ties, and leaned her over the railing with her breasts exposed, and her famous bottom towards him. He slipped off his belt, and with one stroke after another, he left a row of warm stripes on her flesh. She cried out in ecstasy with every crack, and from the terrace of the bistro downstairs, two men sipping *digestifs* looked up, and watched, grinning.

"Everybody can see what you are," he told her, holding the back of her skull so that she could not avoid their brazen stares.

They raised their glasses to toast her, one of them whistled.

She felt so ashamed and exposed that her face flushed. She was sure that the men on the terrace could hear the slap of the belt each time he struck her. The breeze rose again, billowing the lace curtains, and the coolness of the air touched the heat of her flesh where his leather strap was marking her scarlet.

"More," she gasped, "Harder. I need it hard. Please."

"No," he said, coiling up the belt, "You've had enough. I will beat you again tomorrow. Now, say thank you like a good little girl."

"Thank you, sir."

The thorny rose stood in a glass of water on the chest of drawers. He put the cool glass against her marks, and caressed her with a soothing touch. Nimbly, he untied the silken knots, rubbed her wrists, and helped her upright. She swooned in his strong arms. He laid her on her back on top of the bed sheets, with her soft long hair on the white pillow. He unbuttoned his shirt, and dropped out of his beltless slacks. Roark lay down beside her, resting on his hip and elbow, and looking down into her eyes.

She gazed dreamily at him. "You swear you've never done this before?"

"Done what?"

"You know." Pandora gave a coy smile, and her voice got husky. "Played this game."

"Not like you have."

"You are better at it than the master I had before, and he had done it for years."

"Well," he said, with that playful arrogance that aroused her all over again, "We're just getting started."

The second year that they were in Cannes together, they shared a suite at a luxurious resort hotel overlooking the gulf. There were colorful tiles on the floor, and soft watercolor paintings on the walls, and because they were on a high floor, they could leave the balcony doors open all day for the fresh sea air.   Yachts and motorboats sailed across the water; vacationers sunbathed topless on the narrow private beach.   The executives and filmmakers who were there for the market did business in short pants and short sleeves.

Everyone knew that they were a couple, but the journalists covering the Festival kept their names out of the papers because they all understood that he was married.

That was not easy to juggle in L.A., and to her credit, because he had a wife, she had resisted when he first tried to follow up the affair in their hometown. But they were drawn to each other as if it were destiny, and there was no way to contain their passion.

They met at hotel rooms in the short afternoons; sometimes, they spotted another pair of cheats in the hotel bar, giggling over a cozy cocktail, before making their way upstairs. They snuck away on weekends. They went down the coast, or up into the mountains to his cabin when there was snow. On special occasions, he rented a dungeon from a downtown bondage parlor, which offered hourly rates in black-walled rooms with mirrors, cages, hoists, beams, slings and coffins. Some of the women who worked there were always lounging around in frilly undergarments in the front lobby, where they paid for the rental, and they all looked Roark and Pandora up and down, knowing that he was her master and she was his slave. She could not raise her eyes to meet their gaze while she was wearing the collar.

They spoke on the telephone three or four times a day; first thing to say good morning, and always last thing late at night, murmuring fantasies. And there was always something to arrange, to plan, to share, and any other excuse to talk to one another through the long illicit day.

Roark cast her in all his projects, sometimes as the lead, sometimes in a supporting role. Their careers blossomed together, and, because of her reputation, he was considered one of the few directors who knew how to handle her. On the set, they squabbled sometimes, but it was mostly a kind of foreplay, because they knew that after work, they would play. There was always that undercurrent running through everything they did, and none of it was any secret from the crew. Sometimes, they would slip into a nook somewhere on the location, and he would manhandle her, in a stolen moment, with his hand up her skirt, and whispering filthy threats in her ear, and they would emerge and separate, as if nothing had happened, but nobody was fooled. All of the sneaking around added intrigue and excitement to their affair, but they could not help wanting it to be somehow out in the open.

They could not wait to return to Cannes, as the year rolled by and the festival came closer.

In Cannes, their romance was evident to everyone in the hotel, from the guests to the waiters, and because there was such closeness and passion between them, and she was so extraordinarily radiant, they charmed and dazzled. There was a bartender at the downstairs bar, Jean-Marc, who became his confidant, and when the bar was jammed, like it was most nights, Roark could always get a drink quickly. He spent most of the days in chaotic meetings with distributors, financiers, and producers, all over the Croisette, while Pandora did the press junket, with the paparazzi. They were both under pressure, although they relished the whir of activity; him, in his deals and visions, her in the flash of the cameras. By the time evening fell, they craved each other.

In the night, they were inseparable. They met back in the room, and whoever got there first laid out the gear. As soon as they saw each other, they played. They played before they went out, and they raced home to play before they succumbed to sleep. They let off steam. They got close. There was a casino in the resort, and she always liked to gamble. There were cocktails and dinners and parties and *soirees*, and hardly any time left in the small hours to sleep, before it all began again the next morning with breakfast meetings.

He did not have a movie to make that year, but since they were there together, he decided to shoot some footage of her that they might be able to incorporate into a future project. He liked directing her, and she adored being on camera. He filmed her walking in the streets on a shopping expedition, with her arms full of packages, and riding the carousel along the beachfront. She was wearing a white dress with the sunlight hitting her at an angle from behind to give her rim lighting, and her blonde hair like golden straw. He set up a shot of her crossing the old stone square from the church to the fountain, during which he told her to look sad. He did not know what use the footage would be, but she would look beautiful when he added a voiceover and music.

After the festival, they flew to Paris again, and stayed in their same hotel above the bakery in Montparnasse. Philippe was in the capital on business with the banks, and they all went to lunch together at the Drugstore on the Champs-Elyssees.

They ate salad with goat cheese, and *steak au poivre* with *frites*, and went through two bottles of Beaujolais among three of them.

Philippe said in French, "You are not continental, Roark. You speak the language, but you are an American. She is beautiful, but you are never going to get away with this."

"I have things under control," he replied in French.

"Speak English," Pandora complained, with a girly whine.

"You be quiet, little girl," he ordered her, because he knew she was acting up for Philippe's benefit.

"Yes, sir," she said, coyly lowering her eyes.

"I see what you mean," Philippe said, in French, "So, you will never accept my advice. You are both in love. But you are going to get hurt in the end. Everyone does."

Philippe, to show his understanding, told them about a fetish club near Pigalle. He had no interest in that sort of thing, but he had all sorts of friends and he knew Paris well.

It was a French Normandy style building with decorative turrets, in the shadow of the hill of Montmartre with the white dome of the Sacre-Coeur church swelling above it. There were not many people there, when Roark and Pandora arrived, and it seemed much larger from outside. It was dimly lit and there was a bar, and a lounge with a small dance floor. Down a short flight of stairs, there was a wood-paneled basement with a padded black bench and a wooden bondage cross, and sconces for candles on the wall. A strange Frenchman in a leather hood held her down while Roark penetrated her. She looked so frightened and uncomfortable; she was afraid that he was going to offer her to the other man, but he was just keeping her on the edge.

"Beat me," she begged, "I need a beating."

"I will decide when you require punishment."

"Please!" There were tears in her wild eyes. "I am begging you, please."

She hungered for pain; she was so deep in her subspace that she felt numb. He buckled her wrists into padded cuffs with spring-loaded catches so that he could hook her hands to the cross, with her bare back towards him. There was somber music playing, and she arched and swayed, held by the wristlets. The Frenchman in the hood offered him a whip.

Roark flicked the whip and, in a series of criss-cross motions, marked a pattern of red lines across her back.

Pandora threw her head back, with a whimper each time the leather coils touched her.

He lowered the whip, and pressed his body against her, soothing the marks with his fingers. He grabbed a handful of hair, and pulled her head back towards him.

"That's enough for you," he whispered, with his mouth against her ear.

"No," she gulped, shaking her head, "Please, more. Harder. I need it hard."

He struck her again, and the whip bit into her flesh like a thunderclap.

"More!" she gasped, and then through her teeth, one word at a time, she said, "Is that all you got?"

With a strong arm, the angry lash came crashing down. Roark could not help wincing when he saw the instant welts forming on her flesh.

There was a hand on his shoulder, and it was the bouncer from the club.

"You both have to leave," the bouncer instructed.

"She likes it," Roark explained, "She wants it."

Pandora twisted around. "I am okay."

"You have to leave."

It was a warm evening on the street outside, but Pandora was trembling from all the emotion of the beating. He gently put his arms around her.

She giggled. "I can't believe that we got thrown out of a fetish club for being too rough."

"They have never seen anything like us before," he said, waving down a taxi so that they could continue what they had started back at the hotel.

On the day before they were to return to America, they ascended the Eiffel tower together, taking the third elevator right to the very top. It was the most romantic moment of her life, and she told him that she loved him.

As the sun fell, the sweeping panorama of Paris sprawled beneath them, with its famous palaces and parks, and the undulating Seine, and the hulking silhouettes of Notre-Dame and the Arc de Triomphe. The golden sunlight glistened on the river as the dark shadows of the monuments stretched longer in the gloaming.

Roark and Pandora were as high as clouds on the lofty platform. She could not stare down for too long because it made her dizzy.

He drew her close with one hand in the nape of her neck, and the other hand firmly cupped between her thighs.

"Why are you so wet?" he teased.

"For you," Pandora confessed, "For you, sir. You make me."

"Who owns you?"

The lights of the city twinkled all the the way to the horizon.

"You do, sir," she breathed, gazing limpidly into his eyes, "You will be my master forever."

She rented a house on the beach in Malibu, because it was cheap through the winter. It was a poky, windswept place, not in the best repair, made of planks hammered together, but it was right on the sand. That first afternoon, they rolled up their jeans and went barefoot down to the water. There were wooden pilings under a structure, and she dragged him into the shadows split by the lines of sunlight glinting through the splintery boards above. They made love in the sand, in broad daylight, but there was nobody to disturb them, except the white caplets of the cobalt waves.

There was a large deck upstairs, and at night, she put stout candles on the railings which burned down quickly because of the sea air. They stood in the candlelight, sipping white wine from oversized glasses, and looked out at the unruly surf. She was a siren in the glow of the candles, standing at the railing against the luminous sea. The breakers rolled in one by one, the silence of the beach was broken only by the fizzy hiss of the ocean. She kept waiting for him to say that he was going to leave his wife, but he never said it. It was on the tip of his tongue, but he never said it.

He did not leave his wife - not then, not for her - and Pandora did not want to wait any longer. There were other suitors; it was not fair. There were random men who were interested. He was always jealous of them, the way that she was jealous about his marriage. There was something to quarrel about almost every day. A cheat himself, he wondered if she were cheating on him. The whole affair had left them both exhausted. He knew it was going to be over, but he loved her still.

Things started to get ugly: Pandora left deliberate clues, his wife suspected. There was tension at home. Pandora made her own dalliances obvious. He had never been on the receiving end of it, but now he began to understand why the actress had such a reputation for being temperamental.

That year, the third year in Cannes, they stayed in separate suites but they were in the same resort hotel on the bay. They went out for dinner to the Italian pizzeria across from the marina, which was open late at night, and served runny pizzas in the European style straight from the oven. They drank a few beers and it felt like old times, but they did not play together. They attended some of the same events, during the festival, but they were both always busy in conversations and only waved and smiled across the room. They saw each other at the bar of the hotel, but they did not go up to each other's suites, even though he kept trying to entice her. Jean-Marc was no longer at the bar downstairs; he had left to open up his own café further down the coast in St Tropez. Roark missed his camaraderie. The new bartender was thin, pale and obsequious. The ambience was not the same. The hotel had completed a renovation. The layout of the room had changed, drapes spoiled the sea view. All the old ways of being charming did not work any more.

"Why don't you come back to Paris again with me?" he asked her.

"I am here with two other girls," she told him, "We are all leaving together."

She did not say goodbye when the time came to depart.

He came down on the morning she was supposed to leave, just in time to watch the luxury coach to the airport rumbling down the hotel driveway.

"Did the girls leave?" he asked the hotel porter in French.

He pointed to the bus with a white glove. "There they go."

"In tears?"

"No." The porter shook his head, because he understood why Roark had asked the question. "They were happy."

He went to Paris on his own, with an empty seat beside him on the airplane, and walked for miles along the lonely streets.

He was in no rush to return home, to the wreckage of his marriage, and he stayed in Paris in an apartment hotel on the right bank near *Les Halles* for longer than he had planned.

As luck would have it, her photograph was on that month's cover of one of the French celebrity magazines. Wherever he went, she stared at him from the newsstands, and, along the boulevards, there were billboards with her face. It was a bitter torment. The gods were having fun at his expense. He wandered the sidewalks alone, past all their old haunts, and there was no way not to think about her.

He thought about all those nights in secret rooms: the whisk of a flogger, the chomp of handcuffs, the frightened look in her wild eyes, the whimper of surrender, the private intimacies, the quiet bond of trust and understanding. He watched the old footage, when she was so young and beautiful, but he did not feel melancholy. It was cold fire. It was history, and there were monumental marks left in his psyche like landmarks to show him the way.

They met one final time at a bar on Ventura Boulevard, when they were back in California. After they had a drink, while they were waiting for the valet, they hugged goodbye and then Roark watched her red taillights disappearing down the long boulevard. He was tired from chasing her

for all those years, and he knew he would
not pursue her any more. Like it often is
when a woman leaves you, he would never be
the same man again. He would always be her
ultimate disciple, but it was over now and
he let her go.

Peccadilloes

(for —)

ONE

Every story about a stripper begins with the caveat that this is not going to be a story about a stripper, which it always is, and in this case, the story is not about a stripper but a client.

The client was in *La Petite Mort* almost every week, and he tipped as lavishly as any high roller, and he was an easy customer, but what he desired was odd.

All the dancers in the club brushed him away, but Adrienne was his favorite, anyway, and she was fine to see no one but him. The busty blondes were always busy, but she was a B cup, and she was blonde only where she had bleached the brunette tips in peroxide. She really did start doing this in college, before she dropped out, because hey what money was in philosophy. Her only regular admirers were broke twenty-two year olds who were quick on the trigger, and nothing like the odd guy.

He was always polite and kind of shy, older, balding, talked a lot of gibberish, that she just said uh-huh, but he kept mostly in the background.

He always got jumpy and bashful when she came over to him, pulling at his collar and sipping his drink through a cocktail straw, because it was so obvious that he was waiting for her. He was always courteous and lowered his gaze after she made eye contact with him.

What was odd was that when it came to going back into the VIP room for the private dance, he did not want her to dance at all. He did not want a striptease, or a lap dance, or a table dance, or anything that ended in a job. Which, anyway, she did not do. He paid the hundred dollars for the room, which went eighty per-cent to Mort, who owned *La Petite Mort*, and always slipped her another hundred as a gratuity, and he just wanted to stare at her - fully dressed - and expose himself. He didn't touch himself, he kept talking to her like it was a normal conversation although she didn't really follow him, because all the while it was dangling out in front of her eyes.

Medium, by the way, and circumcised.

When the song came to an end, he just zipped himself up, and they went out like they had just been chatting all along. He was always a little nervous in the beginning on the way up the velvety carpeted stairs before they went behind the velvet curtain into the plush confines of the Player's Lounge, and the smell of perfume, but when they came down the staircase, he was relaxed and went home with a smile. He never drank anything more than ginger ale, so she knew that he was sober, but she once saw him walk out into the night air, fumbling with his coat buttons, as happy as a drunkard.

He was one of her regulars, completely harmless, and she never gave him any thought beyond that, but then, to her amazement, she saw him on TV.

She was on the couch with her Siamese cat, Plato, in her apartment, just flipping through channels, looking for a horror movie, when she saw his face doing an interview.

She shot right by it, at first, because she hated talk shows, after all who gives a yackety-yak, and then, this alarm bell went off screeching in her brain: *hey, wasn't that the guy from the club?* At first, she could not believe her own eyes, and she thought that it was someone who looked a lot like him, except like maybe only his identical match, because it was *the guy*.

She always imagined that he was some sort of clerical worker in an administrative post, who plodded along from nine to five, where he put up with being the butt of the office.

It turned out that he was some brilliant professor of the arts, who was the ultimate authority on history, literature, architecture, culture and in all different languages, and he had just received some famous presidential medal for being a genius. He was on TV doing a publicity blitz for his new book, which also received some impressive award.

His name was Doctor Stepan Winston, who, besides knowing every fact ever established, Adrienne knew for a fact, liked to have a conversation in a dingy cubbyhole with his private parts exposed.

Who lived for it. And the hell with civilization.

She did not mean the hell with civilization.

What she meant - philosophically - was how did such an upstanding citizen risk it all because he could not control his impulses? Not matter what. She wondered if he was a Gemini, who could exist in dual identities, like mythological twins. Half professor half pervert. Maybe we were all existing in myriad dualities, in different dimensions, like it was all a science fiction movie where you don't know the twist until the end. *They were in a parallel universe!* And what value should his grand accomplishments factor against his trespasses, even if people found them gross? What she meant was could he be forgiven?

Was civilization large enough to embrace such a vicious mole of nature?

Should he be forgiven? Could just anyone be forgiven, or were there special dispensations for individuals? What she was getting to - logically - was should he, a man of such stellar virtues to weigh against his nasty sins, be forgiven?

She had an idea about that, but she needed to consider it.

Adrienne did not for one minute think of abusing her discretion with respect to his confidential conduct, or capitalize on it in any way. She expected that he would just continue to be her client. She mostly found the whole escapade amusing.

But here was the thing. If she recognized him, others might spot him too. It could be another one of the dancers, who were not so well-disposed or even one of the patrons. She got to thinking that it would be a terrible thing if his foibles got out, and she did not want to end up a national joke in the tabloids either, so the best thing for him was for her to cut him off. End it. Just tell him he can't come back, and, in any case, none of the other girls liked him, so that would be it. She rehearsed in her head how she would break it to him, and cut him off.

Then she got to thinking that wait a minute, he wasn't just going to give it up, he would turn elsewhere. If she cut him off, one of those other girls could get hold of him, and get their hooks in, and they would take him to the cleaners when they figured out how to hurt him.

She did not want to see that. She sort of wanted to protect him, although she did not know why it was her responsibility. Damn, didn't he have a family or something?

TWO

He did.

He had a family.

Adrienne started reading up on his biography, Dr Stepan Winston, which was everywhere she searched. In case it wasn't enough that he was a genius, it turned out he also did all sorts of free work for charities, like teaching and public lectures, and had raised his daughter single-handed after losing his wife in a car accident, shortly after their only child was born. He came from humble roots, ascending the ladder on brilliance alone, and had published a number of books, and received countless awards in recognition of his erudite contributions.

And he liked sticking it out of his pants.

But that part was not in the biographies.

She could not believe that she was in possession of such a deadly secret.

Instead of getting swept away on that rush of power, Adrienne was awed at the burden of such of responsibility. It horrified her, she wished she did not know what she knew, and was compelled to keep bottled up. She ached to tell somebody. It was so overwhelming that she longed for the alleviation of shouting it into the air, perhaps in a deserted forest, where nobody could hear. Or whisper it into a hole in the ground where only the wind could carry it. *The king has donkey's ears!* She wished she had not been the one chosen to haul it around, like some enchanted talisman, but, in another way, she was relieved because she was the right person. She felt that she had to guard that mystery. She carried it around in her mind as if she were cradling an egg in her palms. She understood that if his reputation were soiled, his identity would crack. *The emperor has no clothes!* She felt that his life was in her hands, and decided that Dr Stepan Winston was a noble cause, and she would do everything she could to protect him.

In that, in the first place, she forgave him because he was innocent.

She forgave him, not because he was a noble man, or a brilliant man, but because he was a fellow human being, with flaws, like every other human being. Everyone deserved a second chance, a covert life, an alternate identity. Everyone wandered into the margins from time to time, one way or another.

Hell, Adrienne thought, she was a stripper. It had not turned out so badly for her. She had her apartment, and her cat, and money saved, and let's face it, she liked the attention and the admiration she received when she strutted around stark naked. In a way, she sympathized because she had the same sort of kink. She could understand. The bravado, the liberation, the shock value. Who was she to throw stones? Who was she to judge, as a participant in the act? Or should she say, who was she to judge, as a witness?

Besides, what stimulated him was not that strange. Adrienne thought about some of the requests she had heard. There was a man who used to come in and confess all his depraved cravings to her in a low, guttural hiss, as if she were a priest to offer absolution. *In nomine spiritus sancti.* Everyone had his own journey to salvation. One time after lunch, bending over and wagging her rump, she could not hold back a pungent bubble of gas, and there was a customer who was so gratified that he gave her an extra fifty dollars. *Phew!* One character was obsessed with crushing

and wanted to watch her stamp on frogs.
And when she refused, he suggested kittens.
*If I wasn't going to crush frogs, I'm not
stomping on any kittens!*

So what, if Dr Stepan Winston liked
to go commando in an arcane hole where he
would bother exactly nobody, where he could
do whatever he desired in the privacy of his
own imagination.

It was all too much to ponder, not
just on a metaphysical level, but also, on
the most temporal. Adrienne felt that she
was in a race against the clock.

He had been hidden behind the ivy of
academia before, but now, with a publicity
tour, he had suddenly become much more
recognizable. There were magazine covers,
interviews, promotions, book signings. It
seemed to Adrienne that she saw his face
everywhere.

He had not been into the club, since
she saw him on TV, so perhaps he had decided
to lay low, she considered, but then she
realized that was a stupid thought. He was
addicted. He would be back, sooner or later,
and, sooner or later, one of those other
girls would figure it out, and a scandal
would brew.

She pictured how they would gossip
in their catty way when they found out, and
then somebody in the dressing room would
make a malicious joke to test the waters,
and a greedy conspiracy would hatch. *We*

should get it on video. We should sell it. This could make us rich.

She wanted to defend him, and knew that she needed an ally. Of course, there was nobody in her world who could be trusted with such a secret. Adrienne could not even tell her mother and her sister who she talked to all the time, because the one thing on earth that she had not revealed to them was that she was stripping.

She did not think that they would understand.

It would have to be someone in his world.

Of course, she did not know anyone in his world. There was only one person who came to mind.

Adrienne resolved to track down his daughter.

She would be around thirty by now, and, clearly based on their history and what Adrienne could glean from her research, they would be close.

Aha. So, how to track down the daughter?

THREE

The book signing was heavily advertised, and there was a line of admirers outside waiting to get in, but it was inching ahead as everyone shuffled into place.

The bookstore, the flagship of a major chain, was in a mall, where under a soaring ceiling, there were three floors of bookshelves, with escalators carrying people up and down, and rows of books where readers were browsing. Everything smelled of paper. People spoke in such low, respectful voices that she could hear classical music playing in the background. On the bottom floor, as you came in, there was a sign on an easel pointing the way to where Dr Stepan Winston would be giving a reading from his book of essays, *Broken Heroes*, a critical collection examining the moral flaws of eminent historical figures, from David to Kennedy. A smiling photograph of Dr Stepan Winston was on the sign, and *yep, that was him.*

Whatever happened, Adrienne did not want him to see her. She kept her gray hoodie over her face, and her head down without making eye contact with anyone, which was not hard to do in a bookstore. She was not wearing any make-up. She looked very different to how he was accustomed to seeing her, all glam, with streaky rock star eye-shadow and varnished lips.

This was a different element. He would be shocked to discover her there, and she did not know how he might react. She did not want to embarrass him. She was a professional. She was paid for her discretion. She would never acknowledge a client if she ran into him outside the club. In any case, she was not here to see him, she was here to see his daughter.

Adrienne had studied a picture of her, and tried to spot her somewhere in the room. She did not see her, there were too many people about.

Dr Stepan Winston was introduced by a soft-spoken woman from the bookstore, and, to enthusiastic applause, he came to the microphone on a raised platform with a podium in the center.

His voice sounded different than Adrienne was used to hearing him. With her, in their upstairs alcove, it was all mumbles, and meaninglessness, but, in this setting, his voice over the loudspeaker was warm and comforting, with a gentle sense of humor.

She half wanted to hear out his presentation, but there was the danger that he could scan the room and pinpoint her - *BAM!* - blinded cold in the middle of his reading. More importantly, she had a plan to execute, which is what she was doing there in the first place.

She slipped away from where the reading was happening, and went to the other side of the store, where there was the women's restroom.

She was pretty sure that, sooner or later, the daughter, who name was Emma, would have to use the facilities.

Adrienne surveyed the place. It was spotlessly clean, with tiles as white as paper, and there was nobody inside. She stared at her face in the mirror, and she thought about staring at her face in the dressing room mirror at the club, all dotted with stage lights, and how different she appeared in each context, and she felt confident that she would not be easily identified. She puzzled over which reflection was the real her, the painted projection of her rockstar persona, from the deep well of her subconscious, or the pale, basic canvas which revealed nothing of her personality. She decided that she was many parts, which were not as great as the sum. She washed her hands, then she went back out to linger among a row of books, waiting for Emma to show up.

Sure enough, it was a safe bet. It did not take long.

As soon as she laid eyes on her, Adrienne approached her. "Excuse me...Emma Winston?"

She was above average height, with chestnut hair, and dressed in a cream-colored business suit. "Yes. That's me."

"Hi. My name's Adrienne." She had practiced what she would say. She did not want to come across like she was a crazy fan, or some sort of stalker. "You don't know me, but your father knows me."

"Oh. Well, hi." She put out her hand.

Adrienne took her hand, and used the opportunity to pull her a little closer. She had to get to the point fast to hold her attention. "I know that this is not the time or place. But I would like to talk to you about a personal matter of a sensitive nature."

"Oh. Relating to...?"

"Relating to your father."

At that moment, a woman with a pointy face interrupted them. "Emma? Are you ready?"

In the background, they could hear that the reading was coming to an end. Some of the crowd were already shuffling over, hardbacks in hand, to line up to have their books signed.

"Yes, I'll be right with you," Emma said, holding up her flat palm to the woman like *go away,* "Look, Adrienne..."

"I know your father," Adrienne emphasized, "It's something private. About him."

"Call me," Emma said, handing her a card, "We'll set something up to talk in confidence."

Emma went into the restroom, and Adrienne did not want to be lingering when she came out, or run into the risk of encountering Dr Stepan Winston. She scurried out of the bookstore without looking back, and her hood pulled over her head, like she had just robbed the place.

Adrienne could not help smiling to herself. She had made contact. She felt that she had accomplished something in her mission to protect him, and she was relieved that she avoided having an encounter with him.

But then, he came into the club.

FOUR

It was a few nights later, and she had not worked for a while, but Adrienne decided to do a shift. The place was busy, with two bachelor parties, and the regular weekend crowd, and she was having a good night, with some easy tips, a slick deejay playing the right music, and everybody in a loose mood, with drinks and dollars floating around, and she did not think about him at all. Then she saw him, standing at the wall, where there was a long counter to put bottles and glasses, and he was beaming at her.

Now what? She did not know if she should go on as if nothing had happened, or if she should confess to him that she knew everything, about who he was, about the visit to the bookstore, and the upcoming appointment with his daughter. Adrienne was not a good liar; she was a down-to-earth person who liked to be straight with people. She wanted to yell *Hello Doctor Winston!* Of course, she did not want him to feel threatened, and she did not want to embarrass him, although one would think how was that possible given that she was used to him presented in all his unashamed glory.

But this was where they were supposed to be. This was not a bookstore, or a lecture hall.

This was their domain, the territory that had been staked out before, these were the rules that were laid down, this was their tryst.

She decided to just play it out exactly the way they had played it a dozen times.

She caught his eye, and walked towards him, and he looked away shyly, dropping his head.

"Well, hello mister," she purred, coming in close enough for him to get a whiff of her perfume.

"Hello, Adrienne. Are you busy or do you have to go on stage or anything?" He was trying to appear nonchalant, stirring a swivel stick in his ginger ale as if it were a cocktail. "Otherwise, I can wait. But, I would like to take you into the Player's Lounge, if you can, if it's possible."

"Sure," she said, "Go and get a voucher from Mortimer."

"Splendid!" *Like a puppy about to ride in the car.*

"I'll meet you over by the staircase." Adrienne said it austerely, but she gave a little smile, luring him halfway into the fantasy. It was seductive to him, but it came so naturally to her as part of the job, or, more politely, the persona. She could see that he was giddy with anticipation.

He went to pay the cashier, and she walked over to the grand stairway to wait for him. She saw him waiting in the line at the booth with his money in his hand, and could hardly imagine that this was the same illustrious personage who was standing at the podium to polite applause. The hand holding the money had shaken hands with the President. Among other things. For the first time that she could ever remember, Adrienne did not think that she could go through with it. Oh, she would do it. She would be a professional, she could go through the motions. The show must go on. She would not break his precious heart. But, for the first time, she felt a personal connection to him.

He did not know what she did know. *Like an eye in the sky watching over the players.* Knowing his intimate life as well as his public persona made her feel off-kilter. She did not like having an advantage over him, but it stirred up her instincts.

Adrienne was consumed with a mystical premonition that he was heading for a disaster, and she was in a desperate panic to defend him from it.

She was his guardian, and perhaps, she wondered, beyond that, she was his muse. Who knew what inspired a man of such distinguished accomplishments, and what inner workings, polarities and energy drove that engine? All she knew was that what they did in the den of fantasy was essential to his reality. She could prove this as a logical fact because there was such a high element of risk.

And why did he feel the need to come in to a strip club so soon after the acclaimed reading at the bookstore? Was he on some sort of a buzz after all that attention? Was this his way of letting off steam? Was he on a self-destructive mission? And why her?

She felt a vital sense of purpose in her role, like a courtesan of old, like the woman behind the throne. Her comfort, her appeal, her sparkle of charm, her nurturing, her tolerance and understanding were the values that nourished growth, confidence, excitement and a kind of quiet romance. She imagined his drab existence without her. She was the only passion out of his loneliness.

Under the spotlight, there was a dancer on the stage gyrating lithely around the pole, as a blue mist of dry ice rose around her high boots, and music swelled, under the sublime touch of the skillful deejay who had dropped from heaven.

Adrienne swayed to the rhythm of the music.

They were all cogs in a turning wheel, she considered, her influence on him provoked his industry, and so, in some way, she felt that she deserved some credit for his achievements. She was sure that he could not be a genius without her.

Striking a pose, she watched him approach. He had an eager, puppy-dog look, scampering towards her so as not to keep her waiting, full of expectation.

She took his hand, as was the custom, and led him up the arching velvet-carpeted stairway towards the Player's Lounge. Palm to palm, as was the custom, a hundred dollar bill was tactfully exchanged.

One of her favorite songs started playing as they mounted the stairs to the upper level together, and, flicking back her hair, she pretended to herself that she was a rock star going onto the stage to perform in front of a stadium crowd.

In the privacy behind the curtain, with the haze of soft lighting and soft fragrance, she did not allow the slightest indiscretion in their conversation, kept her poise, and conducted herself exactly as she always did, leaving her vulnerable charge full of inspiration.

FIVE

Her plan was moving right ahead.

Adrienne was pleased with the way it had worked out with the professor at the strip club, which was clearly the title of this chapter of her life story, especially because of the drama of the extraction in which she had got him in and out of there in record time, the better to limit his exposure. *Practically invisible.* No harm for now. But, even so, there he was out on the high wire, daring the world to shake the pole. She had a sense of an impending catastrophe, and she woke before the wake-up music mix on the day of her appointment with Emma.

Emma Winston had an office in a high-rise building downtown, and there was a place on her block where they served salads and sandwiches, which was where Adrienne was supposed to meet her.

With light traffic and pedestrians going by outside, Adrienne sat at a window table, so that she would be able to see Emma approaching.

The place where they were meeting was one of those upscale chains. Adrienne was wearing her hoodie, and trying to keep it all on the down low. She had arrived early, because she was not familiar with the neighborhood, which was full of corporate people.

Adrienne was not expecting Emma to have her child with her.

"This is my daughter, Liza," Emma explained, running her fingers through the girl's russet curls, as she sat with the toddler on her lap, "There is a child-care facility in the building, so I get to share my lunch with her. It's one of the perks..."

Emma was dressed in her same style of business suit that she had worn at the bookstore, but with the child on her lap, she was all mom, and she seemed brittle, not in the way that she was stand-offish, but in the way that she could easily shatter.

Adrienne wanted to take care of this as swiftly as possible, and, under the circumstances, any kind of small talk seemed inane to her. Emma kind of blinked at her across the table, and tried to bite her close-clipped nails, and seemed as comfortable as if she were sitting on broken glass.

"This is awkward..." Adrienne began, "It is harder than I expected."

"It was about my father, you said..." Emma prompted, letting down her guard, "Maybe I know him better than you think. Unfortunately, that includes his faults and peccadilloes." *Opening a chink in the armor, right there?* "You know he raised me as a single parent since before I can remember.

He was a wonderful dad, and we're very close. How is it that you met?"

Well, hell, Adrienne thought, I might as well just spit it out. *Here it comes!*

The child started to cry, so she waited while Emma fussed with her, and when she turned back after soothing the little girl, the waitress came to take their order. Adrienne was hungry, but she had not come there to eat, so she only ordered a light salad, knowing that she was going to just pick at it, but, probably for the same reasons, she noticed that Emma did the same.

When the waitress went away, and the child had settled down, Adrienne got to the point. "I work as a dancer in a strip club called *La Petite Mort*. Mort is the owner of the club, and he's this short, foreign guy that looks like a gnome, so the name is a sort of an inside joke."

"A strip club?" Emma said archly.

"Look, I came here because I wanted to do the right thing. I don't need to be judged, and you won't be so quick to judge me after you hear what I have to say."

"Not at all," Emma assured her, touching Adrienne's hand on the table, "I am totally in support. I am interested in hearing your story."

"I know your father because he comes into the club as my regular customer."

Emma started back as if she had taken a shove to the face. Her face, naturally pale, seemed to blanche.

Adrienne expected her to try to defend or deny the facts, but Emma stared back blankly, so she continued, "So, nobody there knows who he is, but if one of those girls find out what he is doing there, it could be an embarrassing scandal."

"Is this some way of asking for money?"

"I am not like that," Adrienne said, without feeling insulted, "But people are. Especially in this business." She wanted to get into more detail, but she restrained herself. She could not figure out how to be frank without causing embarrassment. "Especially if it is about something personal."

She imagined him in their kinky little nook, but she could not verbalize it. She pictured Stepan drunk on his own euphoria, trying to do up his buttons in the street outside the strip club. She saw the ecstasy in his eyes, like a pyromaniac rattling a box of matches, even at the mildest prospect of their liaisons. Her jaws seemed to clamp shut of their own accord, but Adrienne wanted to scream *He is a flasher! He is going to expose himself at the wrong place and time!*

"Well, thank you for the warning." Emma said, in a subdued tone, as if she could read her thoughts.

Adrienne could see that she had hit a nerve. She guessed that there were other occurrences. It was clear that under typical circumstances, Emma was a woman with bearing, but she seemed so shaken by the encounter that she kept blinking. Adrienne did not want to upset her any further. "I just think that somebody should know."

The food arrived, and they let the conversation drift onto other subjects, each just picking at their salads, as anticipated.

When she left the restaurant, and pulled her head under her hoodie, Adrienne felt much solaced. It was as if a burden had been lifted from her shoulders, to be carried by another. It was not her problem any more.

It was Emma's.

SIX

Emma already had an inkling of the worst. Like all families, they held a dirty shame too dreadful to acknowledge or address. The facts were a lot easier to ignore. There were households with kleptomaniacs, drinkers, adulterers, whose stigmas were so hard to confront that they could only be faced under compulsion. The Winstons had been compelled by circumstances in the past, which is why what Adrienne reported was so chilling.

In such a family, everyone lived on tenterhooks because one never knew when the hideous secret would surface, and send a shock wave through everything.

Emma dreaded that knock at the door from the authorities, just to ask a few questions from the professor; the telephone call to come and pick up her father at the police station; the sheepish looks, and a sense of fear and confusion beneath it; the meetings with lawyers, and the uncertainty of a verdict hanging over them. Of course now, with his fresh celebrity, it would not be so easy to brush things under the rug, and there was the possibility of public revelations, which is why it all seemed so urgent.

She understood not only what Adrienne was saying, but all the things that she was not saying, and Emma recognized the worthy intentions behind her actions. Emma trusted that Adrienne would be discreet. She would not have come forward - without demands - if her intentions were not sincere. With her background in psychology, Emma was an astute judge of character and veracity, having a keen understanding of non-verbal cues.

When she got back to their suburban house that night, Emma could tell that her husband, Sean, sensed that something was different but they discussed nothing. Emma was a deep pool, who did not easily share her innermost thoughts and feelings. She was not ready. Initially, she tried to go through the motions of a normal night, not because she wanted to avoid the subject - she had to address it - but because she first had to put Liza to bed, and she wanted to get something to eat since she had eaten very lightly at lunch.

Sean was a tall man with sharp features, and she was pleased that she had married him, as he seemed to fit the role just as well as any other man. They had the odd disagreement, but there was never any drama between them.

"This woman came to see me today," she told him, sitting down to talk in the living room when she was ready to get it off her chest, "About my dad."

The furnishings and décor were modern and minimalist, with very little clutter, and everything in the house was organized and tidy to the point of obsession. There was a small bar on one wall, and through the window, the sprinklers were watering the lawn.

Sean was watching a game on TV, but he turned the set off. "Something happened?"

"No. Let me tell you. Nothing happened. She worked in a strip joint. She said that my dad has been visiting there on a regular basis and she recognized him. She didn't want anything, but she just wanted me to know about him. Like I don't know already."

"What exactly was he doing there?" asked Sean, sitting up on the sofa, where he had been lounging.

Emma did not like him expounding it. "What exactly do you think he was doing there?"

"What do *you* think?"

"I think he was up to his old tricks. Okay. You want me to articulate it?"

"Jesus, Em. This could get out of control. He is a well-known face and an important academic. He could lose his tenure..."

"Academia is forgiving," she argued.

"...end up getting blackmailed, destroy his reputation, delisted by his publisher, sued civilly for damages, hounded..."

"I get it, Sean."

"Any well-known name is a target." He got up off the couch now, and walked across to the bar to pour himself a second Scotch. "How did she find you?"

"She was at the reading. She approached me."

"A stripper at the reading?"

"Yes. She didn't sashay over in a thong and sequins, Sean. She was diplomatic."

"We hope. Who knows about it? Besides this stripper?"

"Adrienne is her name. Nobody else." Emma almost wished she had not begun the conversation, but she had her reasons. She was leading up to something, but in any event, it was better to be candid. "She mentioned a guy called Little Mort."

"Little Mort? Really?"

"A gnome, she said. That was the owner of the strip club where she worked. *La Petite Mort*."

"And she didn't ask for money?"

"She wanted to help," Emma responded.

They could hear the sputter of the sprinklers outside. There was an open window, letting in the brisk air. The lawn glistened with droplets of water.

"Well, what do you want to do?" he asked.

Emma thought about her father as a young man, raising her. It was not about the heroism of being a single parent, because he rejected that badge for simply bringing up his offspring, but she remembered the devoted way he had raised her. She thought about the close bond which had always existed between them, because parent and child, they were the only family to each other. He had always been genuine, caring and gentle with her, and with his great intellect, had spurred her own bright mind. "I want him to come and live with us."

The smell of wet grass drifted through the open window.

Holding his glass by the rim, Sean came back to where she was sitting, and he handed her his drink so that she could take a shot.

She had been running all day, and the whiskey was exactly what she needed, with the touch of his hand resting lightly on her shoulder.

"It would be the best thing for him," Sean offered, with a wry smile, "But your father will never consent to it."

Emma always got what she wanted, one way or another, but this was a challenge. She swallowed the rest of the Scotch.

"You're probably right," Emma said, savoring the comfort of the liquor going down, "But I am going to try to convince him."

SEVEN

Emma used to meet her father on Sunday afternoons in a chess park, near his town house apartment, and within sight of the spires and domes of the university. It was a pleasant spot under lots of foliage, with wrought-iron chairs and tables already in place for public use. One of them would be waiting for the other, with the board and pieces all set up at a table, and a ready smirk. The match between them was always competitive, and, before they caught up on the news of the week, it was always chess first. Sometimes, people gathered around to watch them compete, because they were both accomplished players, in an unlikely father-daughter contest. She loved to outwit him, because, of course, he had taught her the game, the way that he had schooled her in Greek, Latin, Shakespeare, Homer, but she could always tell that he glowed in pure pride when she had beaten him at chess fair and square.

Afterwards, they would stroll together under the overhanging trees, listening to the crunch of the gravel paths beneath their feet. They enjoyed sharing their private jokes and reminiscences, and laughed a lot together at frowns, side-glances and witticisms that nobody else would understand. It was always the perfect setting for a forthright discussion as a mild breeze rustled the leaves.

They had kept up the weekly routine since she was in college, and, when Liza was born, Emma would often bring her in the stroller. She had not brought her this time, because she did not want to be distracted from her serious purpose.

"So, Dad," she said casually, as they walked along the trim pathways, "Can we have one of our talks? Personal?"

"*Certainement, ma chere, nous pouvons.* What's it about?"

"Well, it's about you, actually."

He looked at her so vacantly, that she figured he knew what was coming, so there was no sense in holding back now.

"I talked to Sean," she began on a positive note, "And we want you to come and live with us. You can have your own room in the back where you can work, and nobody will bother you."

This was not the first time that they had broached the subject, but she had never been so blunt about it before, and, considering her words, he did not reply at once.

They continued on the pathway, with nothing but the sound of the whispering leaves and the rasp of their feet on the hard ground.

"I like my apartment," he said, scuffing his heels on the gravel, "I can walk everywhere. There are stores and restaurants nearby, and I like this park. And, of course, I am not far from the campus. I am okay on my own."

"No." She wished he were not so stubborn. Emma knew that he would be safe and settled under her roof. "You are not okay on your own."

"Yes. I am."

"Dad!" She did not judge him, but she was annoyed. She tried to speak to him in a firm, calm voice. She did not want to ruffle him. "You have been doing your stuff again."

"That's not true. *Pas de tout.* " He looked away. "That was all years ago when I was on medication."

Emma saw that he was getting irate, so she kept her response short. "Yes."

"And since when is it any of your business? *C'est trop, tu sais.* You are getting into private matters. It's not appropriate."

A gust of wind sent a kite crashing into the turf ahead of them, and they watched as two boys tried to launch it again. The kite caught the air, but after a few tugs on the string, it plunged into the branches of a tree, and smashed, and the boys ran away like culprits.

She did not want to argue the point, and put him on the defensive so they walked in silence on the pathway, comfortable in the unspoken communication, as each tried to gather their thoughts.

Emma did not want to reveal her connection with Adrienne, partly because she wanted to assure the discretion of her confidant, but mostly because she felt that any tawdry bits would be hurtful. She wished that she did not know about her father's indiscretions, only his genius.

She loved him more than could ever be expressed in word or action, and her gratitude to him was boundless, in that, Emma felt, her bounty had been without any limits.

What Adrienne had conveyed to her - what had motivated her - as Emma read it, was a sense of emergency for his well-being.

"You were seen in a strip club," she said, keeping her voice low, although there were no passers-by who could hear, " You are not anonymous any more."

"How do you know about this? That I was in a strip club?"

"I will tell you one day. After you move in. It doesn't matter now." Emma did not want to show how desperate she was, because it would spook him, but she dared not fail. "What matters now is that you have to understand that you have a lot to lose. You are on television a lot. Every time, there is a trouble spot in the world, they bring you on for the entire history of the conflict, the geography, local tribes, when there is any story about some famous person, they rattle you out with six biographies of similar instances..."

"I was behind a curtain where nobody could see me," he blurted, "A strip club is all quite legal under the first amendment."

"That's fine, if it stays in a strip club, but not in front of the sorority house."

"It was just a little harmless fun. *Comme on dit.* I've been under stress with this book tour. You don't have to worry."

"Well, you're still coming to live with us," she insisted, but she did not have any leverage.

"I'll go back to therapy," he offered, as a compromise.

"Good," she nodded, pleading with him now, "But, I am still asking you to come and live with us."

"Mais, non..."

"Mais, oui, je t'en prie..."

He laughed, and shook his head. "Thanks, but my final answer is no."

EIGHT

Adrienne was filled with a flush of personal pride that Dr Stepan Winston no longer showed his face at La Petit Mort, and no other parts of his anatomy neither. She guessed that her message had got through to Emma, and the family had acted. She had to admit that she sort of missed him, mostly because she had noticed a drop in her regular income which was her own fault for trying to do the right thing.

She did not really have too many regulars which is what he had been, and what you really need nailed down to survive in the stripper economy. She was sort of on the prowl for the next good thing, so, one slow night, when Mort called her over, she was curious about what he had to say.

"A guy asked for you," Mort said, squatting on his stool like a gnome in the cashier's cage.

"What guy?"

"Tall, blond, with a big chin, I'll point him out to you." He swiveled around, scanning the club. "I pointed you out to him."

"What did he want?"

"He wants the VIP room. He says he heard you were good. He already bought a voucher."

The client was waiting for her at the bottom of the staircase, with his arm on the rail like he owned the place. Adrienne put on a smile as she strutted up to him, with her hips swaying.

"Well, hello, mister."

"Are you Adrienne? Can we go somewhere in private?"

"Yes. And yes," she said, taking his hand to lead him up to the VIP room. "And you are?"

"Sean."

Exactly at the moment that she took his hand to lead him up the steps, a waitress walking past collided with a man's elbow, and an empty glass fell off her tray and shattered. Superstitious, Adrienne took it as a sign from the cosmos to watch out for the stranger who was holding her hand in his sweaty palm.

She already had a funny feeling about him, like one of those guys who tries to find out your real name behind your stripper name, or lurks around outside hoping to catch a glimpse of what you look like as a civilian, but she led him up the steps. She could sense how he was leering at her in his I-know-something-you-don't way.

Most of the patrons were polite and kind of shy, some were cocky, but this one felt entitled. She decided to ask someone from security to walk her out to the parking lot, after her shift, just in case he was the type to follow her.

She took him behind the curtain, and he made himself comfortable in the big easy armchair, occupying it in a way that made her think this was his first time in a setting like the Player's Lounge. He settled in, like he was on a throne, and watched her striptease until she was completely nude before he made his move.

"So, Adrienne, how come you didn't ask me about who referred me to you?"

Now, that did not sound right. That sounded like a cop, but this guy was definitely not a cop. Cops were smug, but this kind of arrogance came from money. He was waiting for a reaction, and it's not like he wasn't going to tell her whatever he wanted to spout anyway, so she thought, she might as well take the bait.

"Yeah," she said, trying to lose him in the dance, "I was wondering about that."

In the dance, as the music played, she was a persona, which was less about being a seductress and more about being a fantasy rock star. It was part of her tease, that she played naked air guitar and threw her head back with a sweep of her hair, which the clients liked, but Adrienne got swept away in her own world, when she hid in the dance. It was magnetic to watch too, following the music, and it was sexy so the clients got lured into her act, and so the dance could be disarming. But not always.

"I was referred to you..." he said, drawing it out, "By Stepan Winston."

"Who's that?" Adrienne responded, giving absolutely nothing away.

"Are you denying that you have met him?"

"No," said Adrienne, playing it like a dumb stripper, and staying with the dance, "That's not what I'm saying. Maybe he has met me. You know how many guys I see in here? I'm supposed to remember them all?"

"I thought you might remember this one because you had a meeting with his daughter, Emma. Who happens to be my wife."

She could not lose herself in the dancing anymore, so she sat down naked on the stool, and crossed her legs, with her heels hooked on the footrest, and leaned forwards with her elbows together across her boobs.

"Sean," she said, feeling sorry for him, "What are you playing at?"

"I just wanted to meet you, and see for myself. Is it true? He comes in here. What does he do? What is his secret? I'll pay you extra..."

He reached for his wallet, but Adrienne waved her hand to dismiss the money.

"What if I told you we just talk," she said, "You wouldn't believe it. But I am not going to tell you anything. It's not even logical. It's pointless, you would have no way of validating anything I spin. And don't try anything silly in here or those bouncers will break you into pieces."

The sad part of the song started, the part that she really liked when she did her signature rock star moves, and it made Sean sound so wistful.

"You don't understand. My wife. She is the only one he trusts, and she wants him to come and live with us. He has refused, even though it would be the best thing. He's stable around her."

"He's not going to do anything harmful, Sean," she assured him, "That's not who Stepan is."

"I know that he is supposed to be this philanthropic genius, but he's very quirky. People don't know that side of him."

The song came to an end, and the lights flickered to indicate that their time was up. For a moment, in the flash of the lights in the dark alcove, they saw each other in staccato fragmented images like reflections on the jagged shards of a broken mirror. *Her hips, his shoulders, their eyes.*

"You see, Sean, we all know him from different sides," Adrienne said, slipping back into her clothing, as the lights came on, "Almost like he's completely a human being."

NINE

Stepan stopped coming into the club, and she guessed that he must have moved in with his daughter and family, and settled down, which was the best for him. Adrienne picked up a couple of regulars, who were quick and simple, and nothing exotic about them, and all polite and nameless.

Of all things, she kept thinking about her visit to the bookstore and what a cozy kind of place a bookstore was, with it's comfortable chairs, and quiet voices, and endless shelves of infinite learning and entertainment. She started popping into a small hole-in-the-wall place near her apartment, and found some interesting second-hand books on history and philosophy. She became an avid reader, but she still liked to vegetate on the couch, chatting to her mom and her sister back home, (who continued under the impression that she was still in college), or just watching TV.

And then, one day, on the sofa in her apartment, having just gotten off the phone with her mother, she was contemplating whether to pick up a book or the remote. She chose the remote, turned on the TV and found the familiar face of one Dr Stepan Winston.

It had nothing to do with his publicity campaign either.

It was breaking news.

Stepan had been arrested for public indecency for exposing himself in the vicinity of a women's college. Nobody seemed sure if it was a one time episode or if there had been repeated incidents. He had been released into the custody of his daughter after his arraignment. They showed the video footage of the Winstons leaving the court house. Emma, tall, wearing dark glasses, and holding her father by the arm protectively, pushed past the press, and, buffeted by the throng, Stepan stumbled along, seeming frail and confused.

Adrienne stared riveted, jumping from one news channel to another to watch the footage again and again, like a grotesque thing she could not turn away from despite her revulsion. They kept playing it and replaying it. She kept wanting them to say it was a hoax, it wasn't so, this was not what was happening. *There was an explanation. A doppelganger was revealed. A case of mistaken identity. It was all just a dream.*

Then commentators came on to express their opinions. They said that such a disgrace might strip him of his presidential medal. Everyone agreed that there was always something creepy about him, but passed it off to eccentricity. Of course, all of those television personalities led spotless lives, without the slightest indiscretions, and sneered loftily at his deviant and disgusting behavior. *What a pervert!* They said that the Doctor would be a laughing stock and the punchline of late night comedians. *Ha! Ha! Ha!* Lawyers and prosecutors speculated about how many years in prison he might receive, if he were found guilty. Which, of course, everybody on TV assumed he would be found guilty, notwithstanding the presumption of innocence.

But guilty or innocent, in the eyes of the world, whatever he had done was unforgivable, because there was nothing that the world liked more than the downfall of a champion, except the glee of ripping him to shreds on the way down.

Detectives had come to his house, with a fleet of patrol cars and policemen in uniform like he was a terror suspect. Journalists had camped outside, with newsvans, cameras and equipment and they interviewed everyone in the neighborhood. Neighbors were outraged, people gossiped, rumors spread. As predicted, he was mocked and ridiculed.

What if they were right about prison? she wondered, trying to picture the learned man in a cage of savages. It was not right that the world would treat its most thoughtful, kind and gentle individuals with such brutality. In fact, Adrienne thought, it was not right the world treated its worst miscreants with such brutality, so how unjust and callous would be the sentence to such a paragon?

No matter what the sentence, he had already paid for his crime in guilt, scorn and despair, and whomever he had affronted with his behavior would have their deserved justice. The perpetrator would be punished.

She longed to reach out to him, even though she knew that was impossible. She wanted to comfort him and relieve his anguish. She wished that she could lead him up the long velvet staircase to the dim lights and perfumed air of the Player's Lounge where his fantasies came to life, and provide him with the tranquility of escape in the soft, private hideaway with nothing to hide.

There, in the forbidden confessional, all could be forgiven.

There, in the Player's Lounge, it was just the two of them, it was their little secret, in the real space which men and women inhabit where the fantasy was the truth, and everything beyond it's perimeters in the outside world was a fiction. How soothing it was to make the quotidian world, the world of harsh reality, just go away for a while.

She imagined the cruel shame that the family must be suffering, withdrawn and in seclusion, and because she had been his chosen protector, she burned with chagrin at her failed cause. The scandal that she had dreaded, had anticipated, had tried so hard to prevent, had come to pass. His vaunted reputation was in tatters. He would be remembered for nothing but his fall. Like one of his beloved ancient cities, his life was ruined.

TEN

He pled guilty to a misdemeanor charge of causing a disturbance, and, at sentencing, Dr Stepan Winston was remanded into the custody of his daughter, and once again, they showed the footage on TV, but he didn't look so forlorn this time probably because he understood that the court had sentenced him to go home.

Oh, and the President did not confiscate his medal, and all the universities issued statements of support, signed by many professors, which made Adrienne wonder how many of those had their own peccadilloes.

Hmm. Assumption of innocence.

The news media turned their focus on fresher scandals, and Dr Stepan Winston faded from the headlines.

She tried not to think about him any more, and she was over it, when Mort called her in, and said a package had been delivered there with her name on it.

It was a copy of his book - which she eventually read and thought was brilliant - and it was signed *To Adrienne, fondly Stepan.* She guessed Emma must have told him about their connection and this was a kind of thank you or recognition or whatever, but she did not know how to feel about it. Bittersweet, was probably the word, whatever that meant.

She couldn't save him. In the end, she couldn't save him, but Adrienne did not know why it was supposed to be her job to save him in the first place. She did not have the power or the obligation.

She worked out that the reason that she couldn't save him, and the reason why it was not her task was the same. He was responsible for himself.

She had seen it coming, and she had tried to give a warning to people that cared about him.   They were not able to save him either. But then she started thinking what if he had just kept showing up at the club, and wouldn't that relieve him of his impulses in a discreet way, under the auspices of a professional in a way that was more acceptable to society.

She tried not to think about him any more, and she made peace with his fall, but not her sense of culpability in it, which mercurially ranged from immense to inconsequential.

Maybe somehow this whole interlude with Dr Stepan Winston and all his credentials and achievements had this impact on her, so here was the thing.   It was not as if she was down on herself for stripping because she loved it: she liked the easy money, and the music, and the sparkle of being a make believe rock star, and yes, being naked, and the fact that she could be her own boss after she paid the rent to Mort which was the first three dances.   So, she was not going to stop stripping, forget that noise. That was not the way this story ended.

But, it had to be memorialized that Dr Stepan Winston, this huge intellect who was so pivotal, was attracted to her, and Adrienne found that inspiring.   *And what had been her major in college? Humanities.* That was what energized her, and she decided that she would turn the other way now, with respect to philosophy, and go from stripping back to being a college student, which was maybe the first time that had ever happened in the history of civilization.

Because The Night

(for -)

When the phone rang on her private line, Ray knew to keep his mouth shut. Louise would look at him - sometimes there was that slight roll of her dark eyes - and she would give a quiet smile and answer it in her husky voice.

"Yes, this is she."

They could be having dinner at a restaurant, or at the apartment watching TV, and the jingle of *Money* would signal the private line - making her stop in mid-sentence - and he would watch her shudder into her persona.

He kept his mouth shut while she was on the call, but he heard everything. Sometimes, she would cut their evening short, and sometimes, to his relief, she would explain to the caller that she was busy for the night. He always hoped she would turn down the booking.

Ray did not quibble, everyone needed to make a living. He did not live from her earnings, he had a job at a graphics place nearby in the arts district. Sex workers were normal people, just like anybody else, but that was their profession.

When she accepted the appointment, she did not change back from her persona, after she had hung up the phone with the client. She was someone else than she had been ten minutes before. Louise did not like it when Ray used her real name while she was transforming into her role. She got edgy around him, because of course, he knew exactly every thing that she was up to.

What she was up to - mostly - was providing for herself, and her daughter; Ray loved them both, and he always cared for the child, when she absent.

He never asked about her encounters, but sometimes she shared some stories, which were funny, or weird, or intense. When she was out on call, it was not his business to check up on her, there were agencies for that. But the truth was that he sat up until he fell asleep from sheer exhaustion.

He sat at the window with the blinds up and looked out at the lights of the city. She was out there somewhere.

She was in a hotel somewhere. She was trying to get through the lobby and up the elevator as discreetly as possible. She was venturing down the hallways, pretending that she knew where she was going. She was standing in front of a peephole, knowing that she was being inspected. She was inside a hotel room.

The idea was to have some fun, being illicit. He did not care about the sex, because it was not about the sex. The thrill was in the adventure, and the quick score of easy money. It was like pulling a handle on a jackpot. He understood how speedily it could rack up in one night when there was action. Some nights, she came home, and before they could get settled in, the jingle rang like saliva from a dog, and she went out again. She worked in a pack of other women, and there was always jealousy and competition among them, to see who could total the most on a single night. They scrapped over everything.

He sat at the window so he could smoke a joint, and keep himself mellow, with something bluesy playing in the background. He tried to let his mind drift. He could see down across the train tracks as the traffic threaded through the tall buildings of the skyline.

She was out there somewhere.

Sometimes, especially if it was late, and she imagined that he might be asleep, she did not call, but crept into the apartment so as not to disturb him. Sometimes, Louise took a shower as soon as she walked through the door, and he heard the sound of running water like it was raining in his dreams. He mostly woke up when she came home, but, if he did not, Ray would start awake during the night in a panic that was relieved when he turned to find her beside him in their bed. They would hold each other, spooned together, as if they belonged to one another, their breathing in unison, until the morning came.

Some nights, she would come home in such an unsettled mood from some experience which had disturbed her. She could be very brittle and paranoid after some random assignation, and he had to go around on eggshells.

There were a lot of checks to keep themselves protected. Many clients were regulars. It was mostly safe, but, let's face it, you never knew. *And he never knew, of course, but hell, could he imagine!* Not a late night went past when he did not think of terrible explanations until the relief when she called him from her Mommy line.

Other than psychos, pimps, robbers and assorted creeps, the real danger out there was from the police.

The Vice Squad always set up stings, and it was a messy and unpleasant business. But if she ever got arrested, she would call.

If she were arrested, the police would have to allow her to use the phone, and she would let him know at once, but, if she were in real danger, she would not be able to call.

She was out there somewhere. He wanted to bawl her name into the smoky air, and cry out for her to come home. *Come home to me!* He wanted to carry her away, with her child, carry her to some distant refuge.

Ray did not feel like her savior, it was just the fantasy of escaping together.

If anything, she had saved him. There was no life without someone to love. He yearned for her, for her grace and for her faults.

She was out there somewhere.

He heard the sirens going by, echoing through the skyscraper canyons. He lit one joint from another. He tried not to glance at the clock. The telephone did not ring.

The Ditch

(for G)

A harlot is a deep ditch.
- Proverbs

ONE: THE ITCH

When she was a little girl, a terrible thing happened to her. This man came to live with her mom. She never liked him, not at all, from the beginning. He had a funny way of smiling with his yellow teeth. There was a gleam in his eyes that looked like he knew a joke that you did not. He gave her that toothy smile and had that look the first time she ever saw him.

She was almost an orphan, even though she had her mom. But she had always loved her dad the best, and he was gone. He had gone in a sad way that she didn't ever want to talk about. Sometimes, she opened up and talked about it, but she preferred to stay silent. Words made things real, silence made things disappear. But he was silent too now, and she missed him like it would last forever. It made her feel like an orphan in some orphanage in a book, with rusty, iron gates and tall rooftops. She thought how lonely he must be, buried in a wooden box in the earth beneath the roots of the cemetery grass.

Then, just when she missed her dad the most, this man came to live in their house with them. Their house was in a row of other houses, all just the same, and he parked his truck right outside their front door. His truck was red like a fire truck. Her mom introduced them for the first time on the day that he was moving in with his stuff. His name was Carl. He had a loud voice, and he sweated a lot. He wore a red check shirt, which was damp under the armpits, and he wiped his forehead with his sleeve. His boots were muddy on the toes, and he stomped them clean on the doormat, which said *Welcome*. He came with two canvas suitcases, with a rip in one of them, and a DVD player, and some movies. After a few days, they got a big screen TV, and she sometimes liked to watch it. They would all sit on the couch and watch a movie, and that was okay. Most of the time, her mom brought her knitting, which was how she kept her hands busy, and she snuggled up next to her under the living room quilt with the arm of the sofa on her other side.

Her mom made popcorn, with syrupy golden butter on it, and they watched comedies or movies about cars crashing.

Sometimes, she helped her mom make the popcorn, and she learned to do the dishes, standing tiptoe on a three-step stool so that she could reach the sink. She liked plunging her hands into the warm, soapy water, until her fingers turned pink and wrinkly, and she was so proud of rinsing off the plates until they sparkled. Tiny soap bubbles formed between her fingers and floated on the air like fairies. Carl did not come into the kitchen so much, so it was just her and her mom. She liked it that they had their own private hideaway. It felt safe and snug. Even in the winter, when there was snow blowing outside, it was always cozy in there from the heat of the oven, and they made a game out of keeping it clean and tidy, with all the cups lined up on the shelf in a row, and not a crumb around the lime-green bin where they kept the bread. The kitchen smelled like her mom in a good way that reminded her of baking and sugar.

She was happy going to school because there were other people there. Her teacher cared about her, and she was bright in class. She liked playing, but she did not have any best friend. She sang in the chorus at the school concert. She enjoyed dressing up in costumes for the performance. When they were backstage getting ready, some of the girls were laughing at one of the younger boys while he was changing his clothes. It was the first time she ever saw a boy naked. She watched other kids being teased, but nobody ever bothered her at school. Nobody teased her but mostly she was ignored, and she always drifted away in her dream world where she was a dancer. She twirled and soared in a frilly chiffon tutu under a spotlight while spectators cheered.

When it was just about the time that her body was starting to change, but before she had her first cycle, there was an afternoon when something terrible happened.

She thought that she was going to break into a thousand pieces.

Alone, in the time before it happened, she fantasized about growing up to become a famous ballerina, but she did not have the physique for it. She was petite for her age, on the tubby side, but that day she had never felt so small. Everything around her seemed colossal. It was like it was all out of focus because everything was so big. She was frightened, and her voice came out in a whisper.

Carl said he loved her. He said that he could not take his eyes off her.

She already knew that he could not take his yellow eyes off her because they followed her around like flashlights in the dark any time she moved.

He said he could not keep his hands off her. He said he could not help it. He said that it was like an itch that had to be scratched.

It happened the first time in the TV room on the sofa where they ate popcorn, while her mom went to the supermarket, and the Laundromat.

Afterwards, it happened everywhere in the house or in the car or any time that he could be alone with her. Then it started to happen even when her mom was in the house, but busy in the bathroom, or asleep. Carl stayed up late. Her mom had bad dreams so she took a pill at bedtime to help her sleep, and when her mom was asleep in the middle of the night was the scariest time.

She was so afraid and so ashamed she could not breathe a word about it to any living soul. She talked to flowers and told them her secrets. She pretended that she was smelling the flower, but she was whispering in its ear. But she did not tell anyone else.

She tried to hide. She squeezed into a closet where they kept the broom and a bucket full of rags. She lay down like a caterpillar on the dusty carpet behind the couch. She crouched at the back of the house by the foul smell of the trashcans. She tried to be away from him, not alone with him, and sometimes, he went along with it for a while. But all he ever had to do to scratch the itch was creep into her bedroom in the scary night.

She had her own room, which was big enough for a single bed, and a table, and a small bookcase where she had some story books and a sea-shell and a framed picture of her and her dad when they were at a park eating ice-cream. Her dad was wearing a cap. Her toys were a stuffed elephant, her dolls, a princess crown and a watercolor painting set. There were drawers for her clothes. The ceiling came down at a slope, and because she was small, she never banged her head, but grown-ups had to duck. It was a tight fit. When Carl's shape loomed over her bed in her little space, surrounded by inky splotches of shadow, he was as enormous as a giant.

It felt like he rampaged around and trampled her, and ripped her open, and spied inside her deepest parts. It felt like he poked around inside a box where she stowed her most personal treasures and keepsakes, like a robber ransacking a family home. Her bedroom and her mementos and her childhood were pillaged.

There was a window with white curtains, which only covered the sides, so she could see the stars in the cold sky watching down on her like witnesses.

There were blanks in what she remembered about everything that happened, and then, they all seemed to blend into one, and it went on and on, and she did not know how to make him stop.

TWO: THE SNITCH

She did not know if she should tell her mom. She felt so dirty that no amount of soap and bubbles and scouring could ever scrub away the filth. She was so ashamed of it, and she felt that it was her fault. She was afraid that she would get into so much trouble. Carl said that, if she ever told, she would get into very hot water, that was how he put it, but it meant that she would be punished. She did not know what kind of punishment, but she imagined something horrible, like being kept in a windowless room and fed on nothing but bugs and spiders, and beaten day and night. Everybody knew that it was wrong to tell tales. Even if it was true, blabbing was as bad as lying. Somebody who tattled was called a squealer or a snitch.

Her mom was not strict. Her mom was a round kind of mom, with everything soft, and her breath always smelled sweet and strong. She liked it best when the two of them were in the kitchen, and her mom was doing the cooking, and when they were cleaning up together. Curled in the woolen quilt, when they sat on the couch and watched movies, she rested on her mom like she was a huge pillow. Sometimes, she wished she had a brother or a sister, but then she would have had to share her mom with them, and it was bad enough having to share her mom with Carl.

She wished her dad was still there, and that Carl was under the tangle of grass and weeds and dandelions in the graveyard instead. It was not fair that her dad had been taken away from her. He always understood exactly how she felt, and they had their own special code. When he was alive, they sometimes left notes for each other that nobody else could decipher. He was always kind, and spoke in a soft voice, and sang her lullabies at night, playing his guitar while she floated off to sleep.

She did not think that her mom would punish her. Sometimes, she yelled at her, and she had been swatted before for mouthing off, but it was not in a mean way, and her mom hugged her afterwards. She thought about it for a long time, and she decided that she was going to tell.

The problem was she did not know how to do it. It was not the kind of thing that you could just say. She did not know when would be the right time, or how she should begin. It would have to be when it was just the two of them, of course, at a time when he was nowhere around. But then, she did not know how to explain about it. She did not have the right words to piece together about what happened. She was worried that she would not be believed. She did not have any proof of anything and she did not know how to make her mom understand.

One thing gave her comfort. She was sure that once her mom realized what happened, it would never happen again. Her mom would be on her side. Her mom would protect her, and put him in his place. She imagined it being just the two of them in the house like it was before. She started to picture how it would be, when she could sleep in her mom's bed, and they could have eggs for breakfast together, and tell about their dreams.

Still, even though the confession was swelling up inside her like a big balloon, to the point where she could hardly breathe, she was too frightened to speak.

At night, she lay awake in bed, as stiff as her dad's corpse in the cold ground, waiting. She listened to every creak and grumble of the house. Some nights, she heard his footsteps moving around, and Carl came in; sometimes, she could hear him snoring through the walls, but, even then, when he was in the dead of his slumber, it was hard for her to sleep. When she finally passed out, she tossed and turned. She had nightmares about monsters chasing her with tentacles and scissors, and she saw herself with a bloody nose that kept streaming down her face like tears, even though she did not cry any more.

She was always tired. She did not have any appetite, even for her mom's freshly baked chocolate cake, which used to be her favorite. She fell into a mood. She became sulky. She felt sad.

She could not concentrate on her homework anymore, and for the first time, her teacher wrote her mom a report about her incomplete assignments, and her mom had to sign it so she could take it back to school. She liked art class the most, but when they were supposed to draw a picture of their families, she could not come up with anything more than scribbles, and she tore up the painting.

Her teacher yelled at her in front of the other kids, and she never was interested in schoolwork again after that.

One day, when Carl was outside working on his truck, her mom asked her why she was so miserable. They were sitting on the same couch where it happened the first time. Her mom was on one side, knitting, but she had her legs up and facing her mom, and she was holding the quilt. She watched the pointy needles moving quickly in her mom's hands, clicking and threading. She took a breath but words could not come out of her mouth, and so she just whispered.

"I have something to tell you about." She scrunched up the quilt and hugged it like a doll.

"What is it about, *sweetie*?" asked her mom, in a gentle voice.

"It was something that happened," she explained in the same whispery words.

The front door was open with just the screen shut, so that a breeze wafted in, and there was the noise of traffic and the clanking of tools from outside. Down the block, a dog was barking loudly.

"Why are you whispering?" asked her mom, "I can't hear you."

"Something happened."

"Okay." Her mom looked at her, and put down her knitting needles. "Something to do with...?"

"With Carl," she breathed.

Then her mom did a funny thing that was not what she expected. When she said his name, her mom started laughing in a high squeaky laugh that was not how she laughed at the comedies on the big-screen TV. Then she said she didn't want to talk about it any more, and she didn't want to hear about it any more. She said that Carl was a decent man and he probably had a little too much to drink, that was all. She said they were lucky to have a roof over their heads, and food in their bellies, and she also said something about making up stories which is what Carl always said grown-ups would say if she ever told.

She knew that he had been right about that, and now she wondered if she was going to be in hot water. She felt so bad for snitching, and she was afraid about what

Carl might do to her if her mom told on her now. She was worried that her mom was going to snitch because her mom was on Carl's side. She imagined a poky closet full of beetles and darkness. She knew that her mom would not save her, and that, from that instant, and for the rest of her life, she did not want to be her sweetie any more.

THREE: THE BITCH

The ordeal with Carl went on for about eight hideous months before it petered out. She wondered if he had simply outgrown her, following a taste for younger victims, or if indeed, he had found religion and repented which seemed to be the case. He started attending church every Sunday, and volunteering at an animal shelter, where he repaired the hinges on broken cages for lost dogs. He stopped drinking beer, even though her mom still had a glass of wine at sundown to settle her nerves. Carl did not ogle her with the same jaundiced smirk any more, in fact he always looked away if she caught his gaze, like he knew what she was thinking and maybe he was ashamed of how he had behaved. He never sought to make amends until a decade later, and that was when he needed her help, but at least he left her alone.

As she grew into her teenage years, she became naturally rebellious. She couldn't wait to get out of the house, which was a cauldron of such bitter history, and, as soon as she was able, she started getting work so she could save up enough to leave. She dropped out of school, and found a job at a dance studio answering telephones, and they sometimes let her join in on the odd dance lessons after her shift. She could sign up for a free class any time, they said, but she did not want to take advantage in case they changed their minds. She worked as a waitress at a fine dining establishment, and learned how to serve with silver spoons and from the left. Her mom had never taught her much about table manners and high-class etiquette. She was always eager to go to work, and the employees there were friendly to her. They shared illicit cigarette breaks, and covered for each other on the job, and she went out with the other waitresses and the cooks after work, burning up the small hours.

While she was still staying with Carl and her mom, she started bringing boys home. She dressed sexy, in tight tops and short skirts, and wore make-up with a veneer of lip-gloss, and boys were easy to entice. They were always a little older than she was, and she liked them rough and squalid, with dirty blue jeans or a coarse accent. They lounged together on the couch in front of the big screen TV on its wobbly stand. She could tell that the way she behaved made Carl and her mom uncomfortable, but there was nothing they could say. Sometimes, there were arguments, but she just dressed how she liked and did whatever she wanted.

She preferred boys with cars, so they could park in the woods under the arching cover of the night sky, and stay out late. The silvery moon hung suspended above them like a colossal eye. They puffed on marijuana and they drank cheap, white wine, which was as sweet as soda to her. Sometimes, the boys drank beer, straight from the can. They were rowdy and loose and always looking for trouble. It seemed that the price for hanging out with them was sex, but they were always clumsy and too hasty and they never gave her any pleasure. Physically, emotionally, she felt nothing. But, even with all their fumbling around, she still liked doing it with them because she saw how much sway it gave her over them. It was like she knew a secret about them. They were always so well disposed to her when they wanted something, and sometimes, they gave her presents, or bought her drinks, and they would do whatever she asked. She could be bossy. She liked being the center of attention, and, most of all, she liked that somehow, when she was with boys, it made her feel like she was getting something over on Carl and her mom. On Carl, who had violated her, and on her mom, who had betrayed her. On her stepfather and on her mother, who should have protected her, but taught her that the world was unfair, and it was your closest loved ones who betrayed you the worst.

She started picking fights with both of them, because she knew that she was leaving soon. She needed to get it out of her system, before she abandoned them, like baggage that had to be disposed of or carted along into the next chapter of her life. She did not want to bring any cargo of them with her. She wanted to shatter her own childhood memories. Some people had wonderful upbringings in happy families, with mothers and fathers that loved the children who looked up to them, but her parents were not like that. She wanted to hurt them. She yelled and cursed. In anger, she smashed a jug that was her mom's favorite, which she had won at a fair, and she felt no remorse. She did not disguise her disdain. She wanted it to be unbearable. She wanted it to be hell under that roof. She had nothing to be afraid about, and she lashed them with her scorn.

As soon as she had saved enough, she found a place to rent. Even with all the squabbling, her mom was not glad that she moved out, mostly because she had become lazy over the years, and now she would have to look after the house on her own. In the end, it was Sweetie who was doing all the drudgery, like Cinderella with her two ugly stepsisters. Carl expressed no reaction more than a mumble about her leaving, but when she moved out, he gave her two hundred dollars, which she did not regret taking. She deserved thousands more after what he had done. What he had done could never be undone; time could not be wound back to a moment before it happened, like a movie going in reverse, and they all had to live with it until the end of the world.

She got a room in a friend's garage, which was not nearly as bad as it sounded, because it was totally redone, with a wall-to-wall shag carpet and a ladder to the bunk bed under the rafters, and there was a bathroom attached. She lit candles and there were masks on the walls and she draped so much fabric everywhere to add to the ambience that it was practically a fire hazard, and the place smelled like incense. Everyone thought it was cool, and they smoked weed, and listened to music, and did all kinds of drugs.

After a while, she started thinking about what the drugs had done to her dad, whom she had loved so much, and she decided to move away from that crowd.

She did not have much in the way of qualifications or experience, and now there were bills to pay, so, because she liked to dance and there was decent money in it, she started working as a stripper. There were so many long hours of prancing around with aching feet, constant bickering, and hordes of obscene men, but she got swept up in the money, and there were lots of drugs there too, so she fell right back into it.

The strip club was near the airport, with a large, pink neon sign pulsating outside, and gypsum nude statues on pedestals at the entrance. Inside, there were booths and couches and two little stages with poles. Everything, from the carpets to the upholstery, was in burgundy or black. There were colored lights, and hot spotlights that dazzled whoever got up on the stage. It was so blinding that nothing was visible except the first row of men around the footlights, fiddling with their dollar bills, and everything past them was murky. There was an expensive sound system, and she could choose her own songs for her set that consisted of three dances on the stage, clothed, topless and fully nude. They also offered lap dances and table dances for tips. The club manager, Jay, was a short foreigner in his thirties with curly hair and swollen biceps. The standard deal was that she had to pay sixty dollars a shift to the club manager as a fee, and she could keep whatever else that she earned. Jay turned a blind eye to everything as long as he received his cut. There was a back room at the strip club, where guys dropped hundreds of dollars, and, let's face it, with that kind of bankroll, anything goes.

So, pretty soon, she started working the back room at the strip club. She called herself Lollipop, and wore a cut-off tartan skirt and a white blouse showing her cleavage. It was all an act. It was a phony smile, and bogus attention, and pretending to listen to whatever was his story. The only thing she cared about was draining as much money out of the client as possible, and do as little as she could in exchange. It was her entire agenda: to get them in a room with their pants down, and all excited, and her intent was to shake them down for as much as she could extract. That was what she was playing, no matter how much they thought that they were each unique. They were all the same, and her pattern of operation was always the same: tease, promise and stall until the clock ran down, and get the messy parts over with quickly. It was easy, because half the time, the guy was too drunk to know what was going on. They all smelled of alcohol and perspiration. She loathed them, and she always found some particular defect about each of them - the wheezy, liquor breath, the polyester clothing, the fleshy bulk - to repulse her. It was enough to make her want to vomit, and she kept a flask of vodka and a bottle of mouthwash in her locker in the dancers' dressing room to get that taste out of her mouth.

She tried to hustle every cent she could out of them. She led them into that alcove like quarry. It was empowering. It felt like restitution for what she had been through when she was younger and helpless. Faces blended into each other with every Bob and Jeff and Mike, but she could not get enough. She became addicted to it. She always wanted to see how many of them she could work in an evening, one after another, and at the end of every night, she came home with a stack of money in her bag, like a trophy. First thing, she threw all the crumpled bills onto the bed and counted out the tally, dollar by dollar. Some nights, she fell asleep on a bed of cash.

It was cattily competitive among the dancers, and you had to watch out for your belongings because some of them were dishonest. There were often quarrels and accusations in the dressing room. Nobody really tangled with her, because they thought that she was fierce. She did not shy away from a fight. She was never going to let anyone push her around after everything that she had endured.

There were all sorts of spiteful cliques and petty disagreements, and there was friction with everyone. She felt that she was trapped in a tinderbox.

It came to a head at the end of the shift one night with a long-legged, exotic dancer called Jasmine, whose seniority was based not so much on her length of time at the club but on the fact that she was having an affair with Jay.

Jasmine accused her of moving her bag.

"I didn't touch any of your crap, Jasmine," she responded, "But you shouldn't just toss it anywhere, like this is your crib. I guess that's why we have lockers."

A row of peeling lockers with combination locks lined one wall of the narrow dressing room, and mirrors with make-up lights and high chairs were on the other side. The close quarters smelled of hair spray and perspiration and bad plumbing, and there was the thumping of the bass speakers coming from the club where the next roster had begun their sets.

"You know, Lollipop," Jasmine snapped, invading her personal space, "I don't appreciate your sarcasm."

"I don't appreciate your tits in my face," Lollipop replied, glaring up at the tall stripper.

"You wanna do something about it?" Jasmine batted her thick eyelashes.

"No, I'm tired and my feet hurt." She had already changed into her street clothes and her flat shoes. "I want to go home."

"Yeah, go back to your white trash home, and suck your daddy," said Jasmine, giving her the finger.

She did not stop to think, but before she knew it, she reached up and scratched her nails down the side of Jasmine's face.

"Suck on that, bitch."

Jasmine, who was still wearing heels, tottered and - off-balance - grabbed onto Lollipop. Lollipop slapped at her again. Screams erupted, and Jay came storming into the dressing room to get in between them before the hair-pulling and wild blows escalated. Of course, he took Jasmine's side, and wrote up Lollipop for starting the fight. From then on, she knew that her time there was racing to an end, whether she wanted to leave or not.

The cycle of money and drugs and VIP rooms and backseats went spinning around like a carousel off its moorings.

She became disgusted by the game, and the men, and disgusted at herself mostly for the endless rails of drugs, and the blisters on her soles, and her nose throbbing all the time, and her ratty mood, but, like Carl had said, it was an itch that had to be scratched. She needed a way to paralyze the past, and blur the leering, pawing lechers in the close back room under the lurid lights. When she was a little girl, she dreamed of being a dancer, but now that dream had come true in a tawdry way, and she had a different fantasy now. She kept picturing the bloody rake of nails down Jasmine's face. The scarlet taste of violence was intoxicating. It was visceral in a way that gave her a shiver. She learned a fresh thing about herself. She thought about Carl and the men in the back room, and she wanted to see somebody get hurt.

FOUR: THE WITCH

She could not work without dulling herself with drugs and she could not get drugs without working, so the only way off drugs was to make a change in her occupation.

She ended up quarreling with the club manager, because, backstage in the dressing room, she was too woozy to stand up straight, and there was no way she was going out on the stage like that on a Saturday night. He called her a junkie, but everyone there had some issues, so it was a personality clash between them.

"I am fine to go out, Jay," she said, her signature sweet lollipop dangling from the corner of her mouth, "You're the one who has been drinking. You think because the liquor is in a coffee mug, nobody can smell it on your breath?"

"You're slurring your words, Lollipop. You want to go out there and slop about and make a fool of yourself? Well, I'm not having it."

"Oh, I'm sorry, Jay," she said in a sarcastic way, "I forgot what a high class place this is."

"I don't need someone in here with an attitude," he warned, "So shape up or ship out."

"I don't see you crawling around on all fours, picking up grubby money with your teeth, or blowing whales in the back room."

"I do my job, you do yours."

"You're just picking on me because I scratched up the girl that you were banging," she retorted, "I only wish that I had left a scar."

She quit the strip club on the same night as another dancer from the club named Nicole. Nicole was blonde and bubbly, and made friends easily, so she knew a lot of people in all walks of life. They had been hanging around with some of her connections that used to go to this underground bar downtown. They went to one or two closed get-togethers with that group, which had been a blast. Nicole explained that in the group were women who made a profitable living out of dominating and abusing men who were excited by that kind of interchange. Nicole introduced her to a French woman who went by the name Madame Oubliette. She was tall and pale, with long, shiny hair, and tiny wrinkles around her limpid, blue eyes. At first, she understood that Madame Oubliette was a professional dominatrix, but that was not the case. It was explained to her that no, Madame Oubliette was a renowned specialist who trained the professionals.

She and Nicole both signed up for her class.

It was a private consultation, consisting of ten three-hour lessons, broken down into topics, and also included practice with live volunteers, who were available to participate with the novices. Madame Oubliette offered a thorough curriculum, which covered everything that they would need to know to pursue a career. They would learn about different fetishes, tastes, predilections, taboos and weaknesses. They would learn about equipment, costumes and props. They would become versed in the wielding of various implements, like whips, crops, paddles, and floggers. They would study anatomy, psychology, safety, hygiene, verbal and physical skills, and how to tie more knots than a sailor on a ship. They would learn how to attract clientele, and be well prepared to go into business the moment that they completed their instruction, thereby easily recouping the pricey cost of the course.

With her husband, an architect, Madame Oubliette had a glamorous home along the beach with a view of the ocean from the balcony, and a basement dungeon through a hidden panel in the living room. It was down the steps to the dungeon where she conducted the training.

The first thing to consider, Madame Oubliette informed her, was her name. She would need an appellation that could be austere, mysterious, playful, seductive. She needed to create mystique. She had to embody an illusion. She would need a name that reflected - not her own personality - but a persona drawn from her darkest psyche.

After that, she changed her name to Sorceress Lola. She still had a cocktail, once in a while, and she would do the occasional bump, if it was going, but she cleaned herself up a lot. She swore off fast food and changed to a vegetarian diet. She joined a gym to stay in shape, now that she was no longer dancing. She dyed her hair jet black like Madame Oubliette's, and got a modern, spiky hairstyle. She cashed in her schoolgirl skirts and glittery stripper outfits for whatever she could get. She went shopping for a stylish new wardrobe, began a collection of boots, changed the candy shade of her lipstick to a sultry pout, and grew her fingernails long and sharp and polished. She went to a hole-in-the-wall tattoo parlor off the strip for a nose ring, and a tongue piercing, and had a serpentine tattoo inked across her back. When she became Sorceress Lola, she felt that she had changed her entire identity. At first, she knew that it was just a masquerade, a façade that she had to put on to become a character, but as she became more comfortable with her recent education from Madame Oubliette, she realized that she was becoming Sorceress Lola. Sweetie and Lollipop had fused into something else. She transformed into a new person, shedding her old self in the way that a reptile sheds its dead, dry skin.

She felt a sense of liberation.

She took to it quickly, blossoming like a black rose. Madame Oubliette was right, that not only did she feel fully qualified, but she could not wait to try out all her latest techniques. She made Nicole promise that they would meet as many people in the circle as they could, and get to know everybody, and be as outrageous as possible. It did not take long for word to get around, and clients began to contact her through different channels, and soon, she had her crew of regulars.

The fulfillment of their fantasies, Madame Oubliette had taught her, was the enchantment that made them her adorers and her addicts. All she had to do was allow them to project their desires onto her, and play out the role that allured them and bound them to her with a magnetic force that she could not even fathom herself.

There was one caveat, Madame Oubliette warned, namely that the fervor of the power dynamic brought deep-rooted impulses to the surface, which could be profoundly - even dangerously - more intense than in typical relationships.

Passions ran high.

They all had their different kinks and tendencies and degrees of tolerance.

She wanted to explore a variety of things. She relished what she could do to them, becoming more sadistic in response to the satisfaction of her best customers. She branded them with a trail of burns, cuts, welts, and stripes. She enjoyed leaving her mark, like an animal claiming her territory, like a she-wolf clawing in the woods. It gave her an orgasmic rush to bruise them and thrash them and lacerate them. She admired the lattice of patterns that she inflicted upon the bare flesh of her willing subjects, as they moaned and writhed with the twin spasms of pain and pleasure. She wanted them to stagger home, aching, and collapse, overloaded and exhausted; and she wanted them to see her handiwork the next morning when they stared into the mirror with a sensation hangover, drained of emotion the way she drained their wallets. Her thrill was to sign her name in blood on skin. She gained a reputation as extreme, which her followers found captivating.

Among them, there were always a few that she left spellbound.

Among them, was an athletic ex-paratrooper with a five o'clock shadow, and tattoos in Chinese calligraphy. He was only a few years older than she was and called himself Tyke.

He had a canine fixation, and liked to be led around on a leash and collar, and eat biscuits out of a dog bowl, but his real desire was absolute service. All he wanted to do was to wait on her hand and foot. He idolized her. He was easy to manipulate, and his adoration for her made him even weaker, and Sorceress Lola could place him under the charm of any witchcraft. Even though he did not have much money, she knew that whatever he had was hers. What was more useful to her, though, was that he was a proficient carpenter and handyman.

She set herself up at a ramshackle loft downtown, with exposed beams and cables and brickwork; the place was cheap, but it needed a lot of work. She agreed to let Tyke come and live with her at a modest rent to sleep locked in a kennel on the kitchen floor. The condition was that when he was not serving her, he would work on refurbishing the loft.

On the day that he moved in, they shared a bottle of wine, and she told him her life story, especially about everything that had happened with Carl when she was a vulnerable, little girl. She never liked to talk about it when it still loomed over her childhood, but as she grew older and stronger, it came to a point when anytime she got close to someone, it all poured out. She wanted people to know what had happened, and how she had survived it. Tyke nodded sympathetically when she told her story, but he did not offer any response, other than a puppy-eyed stare. Just before she set him to his tasks, she fastened a leather collar around his neck, with a dog tag that read, *Property of Sorceress Lola.*

FIVE: THE DITCH

To expand on the possessive nature of their relationship, one rainy night, she attached a dog leash to his collar, and led Tyke to the hole-in-the-wall tattoo parlor on the strip.

Water dripped from the eaves, and the rear lights of the traffic glimmered in the puddles and street gutters. Couples walked by under umbrellas. Stores were open late, but business was slow, due to the weather. They waited in the lobby for their turn to step behind the curtain, watching through the window onto the wet street, where, from the inside, the name of the establishment was written in reverse letters like a barber shop mirror. There was a wall full of alphabets and different designs, including signs of the zodiac, snakes, spider webs, barbed wire, chain mail, rope, anchors, faces, eyes, crescents, hearts and crosses.

The tattoo artist was a heavy-set, bald man with a thick beard, and tattoos all the way up his neck. Tyke lay prone, with his jeans around his knees, while the tattoo artist went to work digging in the needles and colors, inking a tattoo onto his buttocks, which stated in green, block letters, *Property of Sorceress Lola.* Sorceress Lola gazed into Tyke's submissive eyes with a look of triumph. Under the reflections of the muted colors of the rain trickling down outside, he stared at her lovingly through the sacrifice of being indelibly marked forever.

She told him that he had a special place beside her, different from everyone else whom she encountered. He did not have to feel intimidated by rivals because he was bound to her, as if by an oath of blood, and all the other suitors and drifters and acolytes who buzzed around were just strangers.

The rainy night of his marking was the most intimate moment that they ever shared, but, like the tumescent droplets of rain bursting on the grimy pavement, it was not to last.

There was one client that she used to see who always showed up with a generous wad of cash. He was married, and hid his penchants from his wife, so he could not get away too often, but when he did, he did not care how much he spent on her. As far as he was concerned, you could not put a price on experience. He was a fast-talking sales executive, and his personality was outgoing and upbeat. She knew him as Sweet Willy, and had been seeing him on and off for a while, when as luck would have it, he went through a divorce. He had joint custody of his young ones, and he devoted himself to child rearing and bread winning, but he would hire a babysitter so that he could come and see Sorceress Lola on one night off each week.

He paid for a sensory deprivation session with her, which was mostly about encasing him in a rubber body bag with his head hooded, mouth stopped and his genitals exposed, but then, after his time was up, they went off the clock and he took her to dinner as friends. He was charming and interesting in his way, when she did not have to deal with him as a client. No matter what, she knew that he would always be nothing but an opportunity to her. She saw that as they became more familiar, he became more demanding, but she knew that if she strung him along, he could be a career just on his own.

One night, as she was getting dressed to meet Sweet Willy, there was a flare-up with Tyke, who was consumed with jealousy. She had become bored with him, and wanted her place back to herself. He had tried hard to please her, attending at her beck and call. He kept her location spotless, there was never even a dirty saucer in the sink. His devotion was absolute, one could swear it was love. But his restoration work around the loft was sporadic; he never seemed able to concentrate on the labor she wanted done. She told him that he had to leave, and surrender his dog tags.

He was devastated.

"It's because Sweet Willy has more money, isn't it?" he said tearfully, as he tore the dog tags from his neck, and flung them onto the kitchen table.

"Of course," she sniffed, trying to hide a smile, "He's going to spend a ton on me, and he doesn't even know it yet."

He threw his few items into a bag. "So, I'm in the way?"

Sorceress Lola stooped over and picked up his gleaming silver dog bowl, which he had forgotten, and put it in his hand, getting close to him. "We can stay in touch."

There was a fiery look in his moist eyes that she had never seen before. It was almost appealing, even though she had never been physically attracted to him.

He slung the bag across his shoulder, but he was reluctant to leave. "You're just going to ditch me. I don't know how I'll live without you."

"That's your problem." She did not know why she relished seeing him so broken-hearted, but it was even more gratifying than beating him.

"I don't even have anywhere to go." His dark eyes were brimming with tears. "I don't have any money, I gave you my last penny."

"Sucks to be you," Sorceress Lola taunted.

"I will kill him, I swear. You think I won't kill him? I'll kill him."

"Go ahead," she said, biting her lip, "See how well that turns out for you."

"Then, I'll just kill myself." He turned away, and headed for the door.

"Don't be dramatic," she softened her tone, "You're tough. You're going to be okay."

She watched him storm out, and she figured that he would go and camp out in the woods, because that had always been his hobby and he always had his camping stuff in the back of his van. Ten minutes after he left, Willy showed up, with a bottle of champagne. She was in a cheerful mood, especially with having her loft back to herself, and that night, over the glasses of champagne, she told Willy the story about what Carl had done to her as a juvenile, and he said that he was a father and he did not understand how people could behave like that to children.

She did not hear anything from Tyke for months, and someone said that he was homeless on the streets, and having mental health issues, but somebody else said that no, he was camping in the woods near a lake, and she also heard that he went back into the army.

She did not give him any thought, because she had made the right choice with Willy. It was not like they lived together; she saw just enough of the sales executive, and he was entertaining when he was around, telling comical stories about his deals, and more importantly, always picking up the tab. Of course, too much is never enough, as far as she was concerned. She tried to persuade Willy to take her traveling to a faraway resort where they could relax, but there was always the issue of his parental responsibilities. Still, there was an endless stream of gifts, tickets, shows, dinners and outings.

Nicole was also in a relationship with one of her regulars, and they all four went to a few parties and events together. Some nights, they went back to her loft, and Nicole locked her client into a steel cage, and Willy lay blissfully enclosed in a rubber suit with a ball gag in his mouth, while the two women shared a bottle of wine.

They were both well established by now. They worked well together, watching one another's backs, and sharing opportunities when they arose. Often, they joined in for appointments. They each had the bedrock of their steady devotees, whom they could count on month by month. Everyone needed his fix. There were a lot of prospects who turned out to be unreliable, but, now and again, there was an unknown face with potential to consider. That was always a cause for caution.

One day, she received a frantic call from Nicole. She had accepted a new client who supposedly found her number on a back page in the local newspaper. She met him for a coffee first, at a nearby spot that she often used for a rendezvous. He seemed admissible, a little on the square side, but Nicole took him up to her place. She had a two-bedroom apartment, and she had made one of the rooms into her studio with black drapes on the walls, and mirrors that made the space look bigger. As soon as she took the money, the man showed her his badge. Three other detectives came through the door, and prowled through her things. She was handcuffed and arrested on a charge of lewd conduct. She had to walk down with the vice squad in front of all her neighbors. She was fingerprinted, photographed and held in a jail cell at the district police station.

After bailing her out, Sweet Willy took Nicole to a criminal defense attorney he knew downtown, although he could not sit in on the consultation because it would ruin the confidentiality privilege.

Sorceress Lola began to get jumpy about getting arrested, after what happened to Nicole, even though the lawyer managed to get Nicole sent to a diversion program, and there was no criminal record. The bubbly blonde was required to perform community service, picking up trash along the freeway with petty thieves and streetwalkers, and lost all her confidence on a downward spiral.

She started panicking that she would undergo the same misfortune as Nicole. She grew suspicious, anxious that she was under surveillance, or that she would step into an entrapment. She wanted to move out of that loft. She swore off accepting anyone without a reference. Every siren in the distance of the city unnerved her. She had a sense of foreboding, as if something harrowing was coming. She would not survive the black hole of despair of being charged with a crime and thrown into a jail cell. She became paranoid.

When the day arrived that she saw cops on the doorstep, her heart started pounding with dread. It was early on a languid Wednesday afternoon, threatening rain. There were two armed patrolmen in uniforms, and two sloppy plainclothesmen in trenchcoats who did not need uniforms for anyone to recognize that they were the detectives. They all had these identical, blank eyes, and they looked her up and down, as if they already knew everything about her. She grasped enough - as had been drummed into her under the rigorous tuition of Madame Oubliette - to keep her mouth shut.

She expected to be carted away to jail, but that was not what it was about.

It was about Tyke.

"What has he done?" she asked, when she acknowledged that she knew him.

"Do you go by Sorceress Lola?" the one detective asked, without responding to her question, and without looking her in the eyes.

The second one, also peering past her, said, "We'll need some ID."

"I go by Sorceress Lola," she confirmed, feeling self-conscious, "What is he accused of?"

"We suspect that he committed a murder," said the first detective, glancing at his notebook.

"Do you have him in custody? Is he in trouble?"

The two patrolmen shifted awkwardly.

"We have him," the detective said, trying not to be gruff, "But he is not in trouble now."

His grim expression revealed the purpose of their mission before it was uttered.

The police wanted her to come and identify his body.

The detectives had tracked her down easily enough: after discovering the tattoo on his cadaver which read, *Property of Sorceress Lola*, it did not take them long to search for Sorceress Lola, and locate her.

She had to go down to the city morgue, and see Tyke's muscular, blue corpse lying on an icy, metal slab. They peeled back the sheet, to expose not his face, which was beyond recognition, but the marking of her name in green print, which he would take with him into eternity.

She did not have to view Willy's body, which had already been claimed by his ex-wife.

As the patrolmen drove her back to her place, she sat in the back seat of the patrol car without speaking and watched the world going by in the falling drizzle. She felt rigid at her core, but she was shaken.

The way that she pieced together what happened to them was as follows:

It turned out that Tyke was stalking her. He had been parking his van behind a dumpster down the street from her loft, and watching everyone that went in and out of her door. The police had found notebooks and photographs among the leftovers of his things, and there were closed-circuit cameras along the rooftop of a warehouse in the vicinity. Late one night, the ex-paratrooper followed Willy to his suburban home, and before he could go into his house to relieve the babysitter, Tyke pointed a pistol into his ribs, and abducted him.

At gunpoint, he forced him to drive up to the clearing in the woods where he had pitched his campsite. Tyke dowsed his own possessions with gasoline and set fire to the campsite to remove his tracks, sending up a reckless blaze in a wooded area which did not spread through the green foliage, but was seen from a distance. It drew the attraction of the fire department, who contacted the police after they arrived on the site to discover the hellish tableau.

From the ballistics and forensics investigations, it seemed that Tyke had shot Willy point-blank in the heart, and then put the muzzle of the firearm into his own mouth, and pulled the trigger. They lay like siblings in a shared grave that Tyke had apparently prepared beforehand in the brambles not far from his tent. The police said that this was evidence of premeditation. The detectives also noted that the grave was unusually deep, even with the pair of bodies, as if the gravedigger had just kept shoveling as an act of compulsion.

That detail, and how it was described to her - a hole so deep it could only be dug by a bottomless fixation - consumed her as if she were digging her own grave, standing in her own grave, lying in her own grave, suffocating under the earth, and if she wanted to survive, she had to claw her way out of it.

She decided to re-invent herself. She made a determination to quit the scene and the life. She said her sad farewells to her followers and associates, and refused to be persuaded against the resolve of her will. She sold some of her paraphernalia, but gave away most of it to Nicole. She grew out her hair, back to her original color, and hardly wore make-up. She changed her wardrobe, allowing for the preference of comfort over style. She always had style, but what she yearned for now was substance.

She started reading self-help books, and attended inspirational lectures. She committed herself to full sobriety. She went on fasts and treatments and cleanses. She joined a women's support group. She participated in a sweat lodge. She wanted to be at one with nature, and followed a hiking trail to a waterfall where she sat cross-legged and meditated. She started dabbling in mystical ideas, trying to find answers in different places.

She longed for one last chance to communicate with the two lost souls and craved a spiritual redemption.

Near the tattoo parlor, there was a storefront occupied by a psychic, a plump Latina, named Mariana. There were heavy purple drapes on the window. A musk scent permeated the inside. There was a soft glow from two lamps, and, among talismans, Tarot cards, and crystal balls, scented candles burned in carved candlesticks on a shelf. The interior was dressed as a living room although the burgundy and black décor reminded her of when she worked in a strip club. There was a low sofa against a wall, and, in the center, two chairs across a small round table. They faced each other, hands clasped on the fringed, velvet tablecloth.

Mariana spoke Spanish to the spirits, but translated for herself into English.

"I have a visitation for you," she said in a somber voice, "From a family member who is beyond."

"I know who that is," she said, thinking of growing up with her dad and her mom when she was little.

"Don't tell me anything," cautioned Mariana, squeezing her hand across the small table, "He has a message for you."

The candles flickered on the shelf, even though there was no breath of air.

"To find a way out a dark hole," the psychic revealed, "Always seek the light."

The advice was like a ray of brilliance for her, and afterwards, inspired to an obsession, she recited it as a daily mantra. *To find a way out of a dark hole, always seek the light.*

She made it her purpose and sought to find its meaning in every choice she made.

She volunteered at a soup kitchen, ladling out chicken broth to homeless veterans six times a week. She rededicated herself to vegetarianism, and planted seeds at a communal vegetable garden, which she watered every morning. She adopted a Siamese cat from an animal rescue shelter, and named it Tutti. She took up painting, as an outlet for a flourish of creativity, and started to think about selling some of her artwork.

She spent a lot of time thinking about that explosive night in the woods.

She imagined how it had unfolded in the ultimate moments. She saw the moon and the constellations reflecting on the silver ripples of the nearby lake. She heard the crackle of the flames, smelling of gasoline, and saw the plume of fire rising above the trees into the starry night sky, and the thick smoke wrapping around the two broken rivals. She saw the hole carved out of the muddy earth, a stark and unmistakable icon of the impending finale. She pictured Willy talking fast, trying to convince Tyke not to kill him. The sales executive was using all his skills of persuasion, making promises, giving assurances. She saw how he bargained and bluffed and begged, in the last, desperate plea that he would ever make, and she saw Tyke, full of tears and rage, brandishing the weapon until he fired the fatal shot.

When Carl notified her that her mother had suffered a stroke, she was ready. He was a wreck, overwhelmed with trying to nurse an invalid. Somebody had to take care of her now, and this was the perfect chance to seek the light.

After all, in the end, far too soon, we all find ourselves in a ditch.

A Dance In Three Steps

RAINDANCE

In the whispers of the dark rain, Tina throws back her head and sticks out her tongue. The droplets fall across her lingerie, which is all she wears alone out on the patio. Arching her spine, she reaches the tip of her ruby tongue as far as she can extend it, as the rain prickles.

From beneath the dripping awnings, drinking wine, there are people watching, which is how she always likes it. They are a faceless crowd, she is the only face. They appear as silhouettes, behind the mist, so that everyone is a stranger. She loves to be the center of attention, as if they are all spoiling her with their eyes.

But, there are sharp eyes who are jealous of her command.

Now, likewise stripped to her underwear, to safeguard her evening gown from the downpour, Stoya steps across the wet pavement in her heels to dance with Tina in the warm, sweet, tropical rain.

To Tina, it is a challenge.

She cannot brook a footprint where she has marked her domain.

She is the beacon in the darkness. Tina does not like to share the spotlight, unless its luster is more than doubled. Lumination comes at a profit.

But Stoya has a presence.

The silent watchers behind the curtain of the rain shift their gaze.

Stoya soaks up the summer rain, open to the skies, her limbs splayed out like a bursting star.

Now Tina whirls around, the way a child makes herself giddy for the exhilaration of it, chopping the rain about her.

Stoya twists and sways, and her rain spangled hair glistens in the balmy night.

A glow of light radiates from beneath the awnings where the group is rapt.

The women make smoldering eye contact, like wild beasts sniffing and sizing up the other, weighing power. Stoya moves - every so slightly now - into Tina's space.

They breathe the same air inside the rain.

Tina seizes her, hands to her upper arms; it would be an assault if it were not a dance.

Stoya swoons, they tango, the water splashes around their feet.

They embrace, entwine and their lips touch. Their soaked bodies slide together. They are not performing for the gallery now, they have pivoted, they are in their own private den. Clawing her fingernails, Tina has her by the hair, coiled in her fist, using the tangle - as a leash - to lead and control her.

She guides her into the shadows of the foliage, and pushes her back to the wall. The spotlight has gone, they are obscured from view, and the dilettantes beneath the awnings across the patio look about for new diversions..

But, in the leafy shadows, Tina and Stoya kiss with incipient passion, as the soft rain drenches them, and the raindrops dance in the pools beneath their feet.

NEEDLEWORK

In Los Angeles, just off Hollywood Boulevard, down a sidestreet which will remain nameless, there was a private club on Wednesday nights. The crowd was goth slash fetish slash alternative slash poly, and you had to have an invitation and a special password to get through the door. There was a bouncer who did not take any shit, no matter what your story was, and it was a private club, so there was a lot that you could do, and they turned a blind eye, but you could not just do whatever you wanted.

Keep that in mind, because the bouncer, and his back-up guys did not take any shit, no matter what.

You had to get past them at the gate, because, after the gate you were in the front patio, where there was an outside bar, so you were already in. Around the bar, people were dressed and made up in a broad array of leathers, feathers, frills, fishnets, costumes and many colors, but lots of black. Outside to smoke or get some air, they bunched together in cliques, but all the action was inside where the music was thumping. You went past the patio to get into the club proper where there was first a long hazy hallway which opened into a large two story space with bars, booths which could be curtained off, and a raised dancefloor which was also used as a performance area.

Under a spotlight, a man and a woman in their twenties, both wearing jeans, and naked from the waist up stood close together, face to face. They both wore piercings. In each, at different places on their arms and bellies, like papers pinned together, needles were slid with the points sticking out, and the middle of the metal splinter disappearing beneath the epidermal surface. Into the breast flesh of each of them were embedded small hooks, and attached to the hooks were silver chains linking the bodies of the man and the woman. The challenge for the couple was to keep the distance between each other so precise that the chains would stretch as tautly as possible without jerking the hooks to rupture the skin.

The man was pale, and gaunt with a haunted expression on his unshaven face. His hair was long and dank, and he was magnetically handsome, with a clear intensity, but every atom of his mind was riveted on his partner.

She had a firm body, and thick dark hair, which stretched halfway down her back where there was a tattoo of a snake. The claws of the hooks dug into her bare round breasts above the nipples. Her eyes - limpid, glassy - stared unblinkingly at him.

The gathering spectators were meaningless to them.

The twin chains tight, the man and woman moved slowly, circling around each other, as the music played. They concentrated. They focused on one another, undistracted by the onlookers.

They loved doing it under the spotlight, to be watched by all the crowd, being so outrageous. Whatever it was, whatever was the secret, kink, taboo or aberration, some people liked to do it and be watched, and some people liked to be doing the watching.

The watchers marveled in awe and admiration. The denizens of the private club were jaded enough to have seen it all, and, mostly, done it all. This was, however, one of those things you could not turn your gaze from no matter how many times that you had seen it.

It was like being at a racetrack waiting for a car to crash.

The tension was so compelling because at any moment everyone knew that the slightest slip could tear the flesh.

Beyond that, what was clear to all the familiars and fetishists in the club, was that the pair in front of them fastened together under the spotlight, were having sex.

This was their means of sexual expression, desire and fulfillment. They lived for this moment of pain, danger and intimacy. It was about trust.

It would not work for everyone, but it was everything to them, and their bliss was radiant.

Some of the onlookers grinned, some gasped and applauded. Some covered their eyes but could not resist peeking through their fingers. One man began recording the act on his cell phone.

The big bouncer was upon him, his heavy hand on the man's shoulder.

"No recording in here," he growled, "This is a private club."

Flanked by two members of his team, the bouncer marched the man through the club, down the hazy hallway, across the patio, and out the front gate. Eighty-sixed.

You know, keep the bouncers in mind, right? Right.

But, rapt, under the spotlight, their connection was absolute. As a song with a pounding beat played, the couple revolved around each faster and faster with the rising tempo. The glare of the lights, the watching faces, cocktails, curtains, paraphernalia were all a blur. No matter how they turned, they held the tautness in their chains. They wheeled around each other as their bodies arched. The chain between them strained, the hooks lifting on the flesh, right at the orgasmic edge of blood.

And then, the music stopped. They fell together, close, embracing, kissing. She trembled from the emotion of the experience. He ran his fingers through her thick hair. At refuge, they held each other as if each were afraid the other would have the urge to make a sudden lunge while they were still buckled together. They were both smiling and gasping, still oblivious to any other presence.

A moment of hush.

Conversations lingered in the quiet. A word, too loud, was inadvertently shouted in the unexpected hollow.

"Freaks!"

Loud music began again, drowning out any further discourse.

The man and the woman began to gently remove the thorny hooks and spikes from one another, like nurses for the other's wounds and scars.

At one of the surrounding booths, the curtain was suddenly drawn apart. The bouncer emerged, marching out another offender who had contravened the rules of the private club. Eighty-sixed.

For the first time, the couple seemed to become aware of the outside world. They looked about sheepishly, like they had been caught naked, and, with no more sharp points about them, they fished around in one of the booths for the rest of their clothing.

The performance complete, the surrounding crowd surged forward onto the raised dance floor, reclaiming the terrain, and, the music pounding, they began to dance.

FIREFLY

Farah did not eat fire. Eating fire was easy, because the flame died without oxygen at the instant it entered your mouth, but Farah thought that eating fire was an over-rated trick. Once the fire went into your mouth, the presentation was over, so the whole act lay in the build up to - what she considered - the big let-down. Fire-eaters pranced around to the point of boredom beforehand, with false starts and feints, waving torches about and brushing them across their arms and torsos, to try to build up some time and some suspense. They had to collect all their money up front, because eating fire was a disappointment to the audience. There was no panache in it. The fire-eater was always some bald troll with a shaved pot belly and a belch. Farah ate jalapenos, lamb vindaloo and eel sushi with wasabi, but she did not eat fire. She was a fire-breather.

There was a world of difference.

When she pranced around, waving the torches and stroking the fire wands across her hairless body, she had style. Inked in green to match her eyes, she had tattoos of cobwebs, mystical beasts and the sign of Scorpio. She dressed in leather, which was a faded red - matte not shiny, like a blacksmith's apron. She had thigh high red boots on her long legs, and her bust in a leather bodice with slats so that there was plenty of skin exposed. Her long dampened auburn hair touched the red scaly wings affixed to her back. She only felt half-human. To her audience, and perhaps to the performer herself, Farah had magical powers. When she roared, a plume of flame sprayed from her mouth.

She was a dragon.

She always liked playing with fire. She also liked playing with knives, and electricity, and anything that could be dangerous if things went off the rails. When she was a child, they lived in a rustic cottage with wooden beams and a thatched roof; she fiddled with matches. She could not deny the moist feeling it gave her, tingling like a buzz-saw, in her loins.

When she first became a street performer, she did an act with a grinder that she pressed against a metal plate buckled at her crotch. Working the street, it was an edge to have an attraction that blazed against the darkness of the night to allure the tourists and locals who meandered around the square in the dinner hours. Sparks shot up like fireworks, and it looked frightening, but it was just harmless friction.

Too much was never enough, of course. When you were in the business of cheap thrills, you always wanted to up the ante, chasing the demon. From the showy splash of sparks, she wanted real fiery explosiveness.

In her private life with her girlfriend, they sometimes huffed on big balloons of nitrous oxide. These were not the variety of balloons for birthday parties; they got their hands on industrial tanks and balloons used to store gas. One night, she was dripping melted wax onto her girlfriend's nipples, and she had a candle in one hand and the nitrous balloon in the other. They could hear helicopters through the open bedroom window of the apartment. They were both floating on nitrous, and the hot wax was dripping like blood onto Emily's coral nipples. Farah was so tempted to see what would happen when she brought the flame into contact with the balloon. Emily lay vulnerable and exposed to the molten wax; Farah was solid. If she had not been responsible for the safety of her girlfriend, Farah would have probably blown up the building.

If you knew what you were doing with the wax game, you would not cause your partner any harm. She knew how to use the right candles - not oil-based - and keep them at the perfect distance from the body. The wax would be hot when it touched the skin, but it would begin to cool and harden on contact, so that first liquid sensation was the rush. Of course, there she played the build-up too, holding the flame close to the body, even singeing the faint downy layer of body hair. The anticipation created the fear. The teasing was always more exciting than the implementation.

Playing with fire, there always had to be water standing close by at the ready. She liked to prepare some sodden cloths in case of emergencies, or even just for the pleasure of cooling down afterwards.

On the street, she kept a bucket on hand to douse the torches, and she had a bath sponge that she used to keep herself wet.

She respected the fire, but she was never afraid. She was intoxicated by it. She was a pyromaniac at heart, but rather than going out every night to commit arson, she had found a way to make a living at it. She was excited to go to work in the evenings, and when she came home to Emily, she was fired up, and it took the cool water of kinky lesbian sex and nitrous gas to bring her back down to earth.

The eye went to the light, and so, as soon as she had lit the torches, people began to gather where she had set up her space and music. She waved the brands around, and brushed the fire across her body, as more spectators joined the throng. She could see how the fire was intimidating and bewitching to them; lovers embraced, parents clutched their children.

With her lighters and matches, Farah had a metal can of paraffin, theatrically colored in gold and scarlet. When she was ready for the feat, she took a slug of paraffin from the container, and wiped her mouth carefully to avoid having any paraffin on her lips.

She did not want to hold the foul taste in her mouth for too long, so this all had to happen quickly.

She got the torch up to face level, feeling the heat against her. She arched her back, threw back her head, and aimed into the night air. With practiced control, she emitted the jet of paraffin to catch the dancing flame.

The blaze awed the spectators.

They all cheered and applauded as the streak of fire sprayed from her mouth, leaving a trail of fumes as it rose.

Everyone wanted to see her do it again.

But that would cost money.

"Dragons love treasure!" Farah always shouted, after each encore, "Dragons love treasure!"

Pindick

(for G)

When the Dwarf Queen first brought Pindick to the island, everyone thought he was an idiot. No-one imagined a fool like that could be a mastermind. He had a glassy stare, and spoke in monosyllabic mumbles, and he quickly became the object of ridicule, which was exactly what the Dwarf Queen intended.

The Dwarf Queen, it must be explained, was not the monarch of a pygmy tribe, but she was five feet tall on high heels and she did have dwarfish features, as a result of a premature birth which allowed her hands and feet to grow in the womb before the full development of her arms and legs and torso. Her spine curved outwardly at the top and bottom (like parentheses), making her buttocks pert and round. There was something provocative about her odd shape, and she was an insatiable flirt. She had thick raven hair, and alabaster skin, and, if her charisma could not captivate every man on the island, there was no doubt that Pindick hung on her every word.

From the very beginning, they were rarely apart. With a slight stoop, he always followed a few steps behind her on the promenade, where the island gypsies sold their trinkets; in a crowd, she held his hand. They were both in good physical condition. They made a handsome couple, even though there was about a ten-year age difference between them, and his hairline was receding. She liked to play hot and cold with his emotions to keep him off-balance. She seemed to read him like a fortune teller, but even the Dwarf Queen, who knew how the intricate cogs were turning in his head, could not have unraveled his scheme to take over the entire show, and, eventually the entire island.

The show was, to put it mildly, an adult themed circus. There were exotic dancers, acrobatic contortionists who performed simulated sex numbers in the nude, and a bawdy Ringmaster, and there was a decidedly perverse edge to the program. There were acts with cracking whips, and a girl who did rope tricks, but the stunts which the Dwarf Queen performed with Pindick would shock the audience, and keep them coming back for more.

The theater was attached to an exclusive couples-only resort on a white sand beach. It had begun as something of a rundown striptease attraction, in a musty old burlesque house, but it became a glittering success when the Dwarf Queen put Pindick up on stage. The Dwarf Queen loved the limelight, and, even, in the end when it was apparent that Pindick was the real star of the show, she accepted that fact just so that she could be the one to stand beside him.

Pindick was the circus clown, a sad-faced clown with a droopy mouth, a Bozo wig, and the ubiquitous red nose. He always looked like he was about to break into tears. He wore purple pantaloons with a ruffle, and flapped around in clown feet that gave him a bandy gait. The premise of the act, which changed every night, and became more and more abusive, as the audience came back with a bloodlust that turned into a frenzy, was to improvise ways to torment and humiliate Pindick.

At first, it was just about throwing pies at him, while he stood helpless with that mournful look on his white painted face, but the Dwarf Queen knew no limits. She slapped him around, beat him and whipped him, the lash cracking against any part of his body or his head. She put a bit into his mouth, and gave him a donkey tail, and rode him around the stage, using a crop and spurs to make him trot. Dressed in fishnet stockings, top hat and tails like Marlene Dietrich in the Blue Angel, which was her favorite picture, she drizzled honey and chicken feathers over Pindick, and invited onlookers to aim raw eggs at him until he was dripping with yolk and eggshells. She handed out tomatoes to the first three rows, and, like a medieval mob, they hurled rotten fruit at him while he sang in a falsetto voice. She forced his jaws open with a metallic dental device, and allowed members of the audience to pour surprise fluids into his yawning orifice. It could have been a shot of Vodka or a glass of liquid soap, or sour milk, and, after a while, she would encourage them to shoot spitballs through a straw into the target, and then, there was a squirt gun apparently filled with urine.

But, since this was an adult-themed show with plenty of nudity, on private property, where no-one was policing them, the highlight of the performance was to expose the clown's genitals. Some nights, the Dwarf Queen would de-pants him unexpectedly, creeping up behind him with a wicked smile to the spectators while he was trying to juggle, and jerk his pantaloons down with the elastic around his ankles; some nights, she would have him perform a clumsy striptease, while the men and women of the audience cawed and chanted. As the drums rolled, there he stood shell-shocked under the probing spotlight, with his tiny shriveled penis on display for jeers and cackles, and, ultimately, brutal silence.

This was what they had all paid for tickets to witness.

The Dwarf Queen led him off triumphantly, as he pulled up his trousers and bunched the waistline in his fist. She always had to be attentive to him afterwards, like a mother with a child, or, if the mood was right, she would keep him going as if they were still on the stage, handling him harshly and pushing his face into a backstage corner to wait for her while she went to get a drink. She knew that after the performance, his head would be wobbling like a china plate on a bamboo pole, and she had to bring him down slowly.

By the time they were alone together in their room at the end of the long night, they spoke freely, discussed the reactions of the audience, and thought of ways they could improve the act, or new tricks to perform. Pindick was always brimming with suggestions. She always admired how clever he was, but no-one would have imagined it. Even the Dwarf Queen did not realize the levels to his manipulation.

Of course, any man who called himself Pindick and who revealed his undersized member to the world had to have a sense of inner security that did not depend on factors about which other men were sensitive. In fact, as the Dwarf Queen knew, because of how he had been raised, and because of his intellectual abilities, Pindick the clown was vain and arrogant. He felt so superior to the spectators who paid money to snigger at him that their mockery meant nothing. In a way, studying their responses, he was the one who was mocking them.

The customers did not see it that way though, and word of the outrageous act spread through the island, and around the globe. People came from other hotels along the beachfront, and from towns on the opposite shore, and in the hills, and then from distant lands. Guests returned annually to the resort, bringing new guests in tow, and business increased rapidly. Tickets for the show were sold out months in advance. There were masks, postcards, souvenirs and posters for sale, but the Dwarf Queen was adamant that Pindick could not be photographed on stage. The act had to be experienced in person. On rare occasions, before the evening performance, when Pindick was in full white-faced make-up, wig and costume, she led him along the boardwalk, and visitors flocked for photographs with their arms around him. They always tried to pinch his nose, but she prevented them. Little did anyone realize the sinister secret that the red spongy nose was concealing.

If anyone were paying attention, they would have noticed how alarmed the clown became when a giddy fan reached for his nose. But the Dwarf Queen always made sure that his nose was safe.

Pindick became so popular that a second scene was added. The clown usually appeared late in the program, just before the finale, because there really was no-one to follow him. He was what they had all come to see, and it was the climax of the show. The Dwarf Queen negotiated an additional fee for a sort of a warm-up teaser early in the presentation. This kept the impatient spectators calm, and whet their appetites for what would come later. The Dwarf Queen would not appear in the teaser, and it would be performed wholly between Pindick and the Ringmaster.

The Ringmaster was a big-bellied foreigner in a scarlet topcoat with a booming voice, and a collection of vulgar jokes and songs, which he would belt out into a microphone in different languages. The ruse that they worked out was that he would ask for volunteers from the audience, and Pindick, making his entrance from the back of the hall, would be the one that he selected.

The Ringmaster was a natural to play the part of the bully, and he found new ways to abuse the clown each night. He made him wear a dunce cap, used a whip to crack a playing card from between his teeth, and tricked him into sitting on a cream pie. The clown always seemed terrified of the Ringmaster. One night, when the crowd was insatiable for it, he hypnotized Pindick to copulate with a stuffed sheep. He did not like to tell Pindick before the show what he was planning, but he always consulted with the Dwarf Queen in advance.

The Dwarf Queen did not care much for the Ringmaster, but she was envious of how much the spotlight shone on him, as the centerpiece of the show. There were always allegiances and jealousies among the performers. There were the strippers and chorus girls who idolized the Dwarf Queen like infatuated schoolchildren. There was Jumba the circus strongman, with hairless, oily muscles, who felt deep sympathy for Pindick, and stood up for the clown long before he became so celebrated. Jumba was always bewildered by the way that Pindick was maltreated. There was Wanda the man-girl, who rivaled the Dwarf Queen, but they kept an easy fellowship between them. She was called the man-girl, not because of any ambivalence about her sexuality, but because of her athletic build. She was blonde and voluptuous, and dressed like a mythological goddess, and she did an act that was mostly about whip-cracking. Once in a while, when her co-star had been too soused or marked up too badly from the previous night to appear in public, the Dwarf Queen let Wanda borrow Pindick, and bind him to the post.

The whip, Pindick scoffed in private, was not his specialty, but he had trained to take the lash. What he displayed was more cerebral, the whip was mindless and barbaric. Most of it was bluff and showmanship. There were loud snappers which did not hurt, there were vipers with a silent bite. The trick was that as long as the coils struck the body after the crack, the force had all been shaken out of it, and, as long as the reaction of the victim was believable, the audience would think he had been stung. Of course, mistakes could happen, and, let's face it, once in a while, it was deliberate.

It was Wanda who would take Pindick to the stage on the night of his final performance.

By that time, Pindick had become such a celebrity on the island that he was not even referred to by name. At first, people enjoyed the jape of calling out to him, because his name itself was such an insult. But, after a while, they were uncomfortable about it, and he was called *Mister* Pindick, and then, it was just Mr P, and no-one dared to breathe the real name of the legendary artiste. People pointed and nodded and whispered when he was seen. His infamy overwhelmed the rabble. His antics became less about his victimization than his daring. Everyone had witnessed the show, and they all had a favorite feat which they remembered. They always wondered what he would accomplish next.

He never paid for a drink at any bar or a meal or a taxi anywhere on the island, and he was never kept waiting, and everything was complimentary. The Dwarf Queen relished it, but Mr P accepted his fame with modesty, as if it was simply his due. Offstage, he took to a stylish black pinstripe wardrobe. He started to go around without her more and more, but they always yearned for one another when they were apart. They could not stand to be apart from one another for too long.

This was especially true before and after the performance when they were both in their roles.

They always used to have a few drinks to wind down after the show, but, on the night before what was to be his last appearance, Pindick could not find her, and he started to panic. He had been in the communal dressing room backstage, removing his greasepaint and his costume, and she was not at the pool-deck bar where they usually met. He waited until closing time but she did not come.

He went down to the beach because, on a hot night, the Dwarf Queen liked to swim in the ocean under the moonlight, and he feared that, a little under the influence, and easy prey for the seductive tides, she might have been swept away by the backwash. There was nothing but empty paddleboats and beach chairs with no cushions, and all the umbrellas were folded. He heard the sound of the wind and the breakers. The smell of salt was in the air. He was the only one on the sand. He stared into the black waves.

He checked their room on the ground floor. Their bed had not been touched, everything was neat and sterile. The soft pastel colors and the utilitarian fixtures of the hotel room made it feel like an infirmary, but for the vivid textiles of their theatrical costumes and property. Her half-finished drink was still on the table among her make-up vials and powders, but the ice had melted.

He looked all through the resort. No-one seemed to know where she was. He was filled with a sense of foreboding.

It was almost four a.m. when, without even knowing why, he went up the steps and along the open corridor to the Ringmaster's room.

The door was ajar, and he could tell that inside the lamp was glowing, and there were muffled sounds.

He tapped on the door. "Its Pindick."

"Come in, Pindick," he heard the Dwarf Queen's voice. "I'm in here."

He was relieved that he had found her, and he let the door swing open.

The Dwarf Queen was naked in the bed, her dwarfish body across the big buttery flesh of the Ringmaster.

"You can sit in the corner, and watch us," she instructed.

"Yes, Pindick," guffawed the Ringmaster, "Watch me do her."

The clown stared transfixed, and collapsed like a marionette onto the floor in the corner, unable to take his eyes off the bed. He could not understand why the Dwarf Queen would allow a bloated bully like the Ringmaster to use her so obscenely, and, as if to make matters more hurtful, the Ringmaster was naked in every way, except that he was wearing Pindick's bright red nose.

"How many times has wormboy witnessed you with a real man?' the Ringmaster asked the Dwarf Queen.

"Actually, you are the first," she told him.

"Oh, what an honor," he said sarcastically, as if they were all on stage doing the routine.

Pindick watched them at it, and tried to see himself from the outside, like he did when he was under the spotlight with his trousers around his feet. The Ringmaster grunted out some taunts, but they became so absorbed in what they were doing together, that they did not seem to notice him in the corner any more. The foreigner was too big to lie across her small child-like body, so she rode him astride, and then, he got behind her with the Dwarf Queen on all fours on top of the sheets. She moaned with passion as he thrust into her. The clown curled up into the corner, with his legs to his chest, and his eyes covered, but he could not stop himself from peeking through his fingers.

They finished - for the moment - and then, they half-turned their attention back to him.

He got to his feet, sliding up the wall. "I'm going back to the room."

"I said to watch us," the Dwarf Queen repeated, because she never liked to be defied.

"I don't want to watch." He stumbled to the doorway. "I said I'm going back to the room."

"I will deal with you later." she said sharply.

He went out, and, not quite realizing the strength of it, he slammed the door.

In their room, he could not sleep. It was not the same without her in the bed. They always slept topsy-turvy, like an endless circle, because, restless sleepers, they found they would disturb each other less through the night if they lay head to feet. He rested on her side of the bed, his head on her soft pillow with a trace of her scent. He knew that she had had too much to drink, but he was hollow and confused.

As day was breaking, the four walls of the room closed in like a painted cage, and he could not catch his breath, so, outside, he found a hammock between palm trees where the resort met the beach. He could hear the sound of the waves lapping at the shore, and the hammock swayed gently.

He lay in the curve of the hammock like a fish in a net, and dozed off as the breeze rustled the palm fronds, but he kept waking to the same picture in his mind of

the Dwarf Queen and the Ringmaster.   He
memorized all the words that he would say to
her when they saw each other.

     After a few hours, he rolled off the
hammock and went to look for her in their
room again.   She was not there, although
now, he knew where he could locate her. He
did not want to disturb her.   He guessed
that she was probably trying to sleep it
off.

     He had no appetite, but he realized
that, with little sleep, he should at least
try to have some food. She had drummed into
him how to take good care of himself.

     Lined up at the lunch buffet, where
the performers were eating among the guests,
he encountered the Ringmaster.   In baggy
flannel pants, and a loose shirt to hide his
paunch, and with a plate of sardines perched
on his fingertips, the foreigner did not
seem so intimidating.

     "Mister Pindick," the Ringmaster took
him to one side, "I wanted to apologize to
you..."

     "No,   no,   no.   There   is   no
apology necessary.   The   Dwarf   Queen
can   do   whatever   she   wants   to..."

     "You   know, Mister Pindick," the
Ringmaster said earnestly, "We all have such
great respect for you. We really like you."

     "I could give a damn what you think of
me," the clown said fiercely.

     The Ringmaster did not flinch.   "I
just wanted you to know that."

"Look, just give me a wide berth today," warned Pindick, "Just stay out of my way."

"Of course."

"I'll be ready for the show tonight, but keep out of my face until we get on stage." He caught a fishy whiff of the sardines, and suddenly felt queasy.

"I'm going to make you eat fire," the Ringmaster said politely, "If that's all right?"

Pindick nodded.

"There's nothing to worry about," the Ringmaster assured him, "There is no air in the human mouth, and it is full of moisture, so the flame will die instantly."

"I know how to do the trick," Pindick said, "You won't hurt me."

The Ringmaster set down his plate on a table, put out his broad palm, and beamed. He held it out until Pindick shook his hand, and, the burly man wrapped his other arm around Pindick in a sweaty hug.

"Thank you, Mister Pindick," he said, with a little bow.

"Thank you," said Pindick, "You handled it just fine."

At around five p.m., as he approached their room from the rear across the lawn, he saw her silhouette through the bathroom window. She was in the shower, and the soapy water was so scalding that the steam fogged the glass. Even though he had practiced their conversation in his head all day, he did not know what he would say to her. He waited on the grassy walkway another thirty minutes before he went through the door.

For once, she did not seem to know what to say either, and they both mumbled hello, but they could not make eye contact. This was the time of day when they would usually start to prepare for the evening performance. He would fetch their drinks from the bar. She would do her own make-up first, sitting on a stool in front of the mirror, while he waited mutely on the mat. He would try to concentrate on his role, and lay out her wardrobe on the bed. Then, she would get him into makeup, and his costume, and, lastly, she would apply the nose. By the time, they left for the theater, they would be in character.

But she showed no signs of beginning the preparations.

"Look," he broke the silence at last, "I don't think I can do the act tonight..."

She glared at him. "You will do the act."

"My head is not in the right space. I am not going to be able..."

"Are we going to have a problem?" she tried not to raise her voice.

"I don't want to have a problem. We have had enough problems. I just don't want to go on..."

"You will go on. People are expecting you."

"I have never missed a performance before," he said sullenly, "They can go one night without me."

"You will not miss a performance tonight either," the Dwarf Queen said, her voice rising now, "You are not sick. You are not injured. You don't feel like going on, well, too bad. How do we know you will feel like going on tomorrow?"

"I will get over myself in a few days..."

The Dwarf Queen would never let the clown prevail. "You will get over yourself now. You are not going to let everyone down. You wanted to be the center of attention. You are the number one attraction in the freakshow. This is the price of being the star. The show must go on."

"I just don't think that I can do the show with you," he admitted, hoping to hurt her feelings.

"I am not stupid," she declared complacently, because she had an ace up her sleeve. "I have already thought of that. I know you so well."

Pindick realized she was ahead of him. "Then, how?"

"You will do the act with Wanda."

He liked the idea of doing the performance with the man-girl. He did not appreciate how she always tried to compete with the Dwarf Queen, but he could not deny that there had been a spark of electricity between them whenever they had appeared together before. It was not the same, but she had her own set of skills. At first, it had been easy; it was getting harder and harder to do the act. He was curious to see where Wanda might take the scene.

"I have already discussed it with her," the Dwarf Queen continued, "And she has agreed."

"What about the nose?" the clown asked sheepishly.

"She knows about the nose."

"What did you tell her?"

"I didn't tell her everything. I told her that you need the nose to get into character. She understands."

He did not feel so isolated now. Over the years, everyone had weak moments. Intoxicated, she had followed her impulses and now she was ashamed. She had no reason to feel shame, he understood, she was a free spirit. They could forgive each other for anything. He had the feeling that despite what had happened she was still trying to watch over him. She was always so protective towards him. She had considered his feelings. It would all be easy if he was wearing the nose.

Pindick surrendered. "All right. I will do the act with Wanda."

The sun was setting over the ocean, and they had not yet turned on the lamps in the room. They gazed at one another in the half-light.

"I will prepare the nose for you beforehand." She softened her tone, and came closer to where he was standing. "So, you will have nothing to worry about."

But the Dwarf Queen would never see her partner again after that night.

Wanda the man-girl came to the room to get Pindick about half an hour before curtain. She was wearing a tight spangled leotard, a short cape, elbow-length gloves and high shiny boots, and she had her signature whip coiled about her. In white face paint and in costume, the clown was ready. She took hold of him roughly.

"Let's go, fool," she laughed.

Pindick blinked at her vacantly, and muttered an inaudible response.

The Dwarf Queen smiled at Wanda. "He's all yours. Have fun."

"Enjoy your night off," said Wanda.

They went out into the corridor, and the Dwarf Queen watched them leave. Wanda strode a few steps ahead, with a swing in her hips, while Pindick waddled behind her in his clown feet with his head bowed.

A warm breeze was stirring. The night had fallen, and the half-moon rose over the sea.

It was a short walk through the resort to the backstage entrance of the old burlesque house. From a distance, illuminated, the creaky building loomed spookily against the dark horizon. It gave him that same ominous feeling in the pit of his stomach.

Pindick took his place at the back of the theater as soon as the house lights went down. He had never felt nervous before. He always waited until his cue, when the Ringmaster asked for a volunteer, someone ridiculous. Then the spotlight would sweep through the audience and discover him at the back of the hall. At first, he pretended that he did not want to go up on the stage, and the Ringmaster would be insistent. People started clapping and whistling, sometimes someone would give him a shove, as he gingerly went forward and up the small flight of steps at the apron.

But on that final night the Ringmaster thought better of it. He went through the motions, and the spotlight raked the seats, and skimmed right by him. The harsh beam of it settled instead on one of the hotel guests, a tall, thin, lantern-jawed man on holiday. The Ringmaster called him up, and egged on by his group of friends, the volunteer did the fire-eating trick while Pindick watched from the back of the theater.

Half-relieved,   half-jealous,   he shuffled out through the side doors, and went backstage to wait for his turn with the man-girl.

Wanda strutted up to him as he waited in a corner of the wings, getting her face so close to his face that he could count the tiny beads of perspiration on her forehead.

"Nobody wanted to see you eat fire,"

she teased, "Oh, poor little Pindick." Then she playfully squeezed his spongy nose. "What on earth am I going to do to you tonight?"

A kaleidoscope of naked bodies, feathers, glitter, scenery, backdrops, trampolines and trapezes tumbled through his mind. There was frantic circus music and laughter and applause and he imagined that he could hear the drumbeat of his own heart. His head spun like a pinwheel. His legs felt weak. He saw the blurry features of the man-girl in front of him, her white teeth gleaming in a lascivious grin, but he could not focus his eyes. He tried to catch his breath, sucking in the air through his lips. He hardly recognized where he was. Everything in the grand universe seemed pinpointed to the overwhelming image of the Ringmaster and the Dwarf Queen doing it.

Time speeded up, and, before he knew it, he heard the Ringmaster wielding the microphone to announce the act which everyone had been waiting for, and then, Wanda was marching him out onto the stage, and he heard the crowd stamping their feet, and jeering in unison, "Pin-dick! Pin-dick! Pin-dick!"

The spotlight hit him, and a roar of delight came from the throng.

Wanda circled around him, in front of him, in his face, then behind him, invisible. She prodded him, poked him, and, all of a sudden, she jerked his trousers down around his ankles, and he stood exposed.

"We're going to do the Penguin tonight," she declared, crossing to the far side of the stage, "Let's see you do the Penguin walk."

Hands perpendicular to the sides, he took a few awkward steps towards her. He saw the Ringmaster leering from the wings, his lips curved in a nasty smile. Pindick looked around, lost without the Dwarf Queen to encourage him. He took a deep inhalation, and, in his stupor, stumbled leadenly towards the bleary figure in the spangled cape.

It was not quick enough for Wanda. She uncoiled her whip, and cracked it once against the hard wooden planks of the stage so that the yellow dust rose from the floorboards.

"I'm waiting for you," she said, with a lilt in her voice, and he tried to get his legs to work faster.

Then, as he approached her, Wanda did the cruelest thing that Pindick could have imagined.

She tossed her whip aside, and before he knew it, she reached for his face, and, in a flash, she had plucked off his nose.

"No!" cried the clown.

The audience erupted with laughter.

"You want it," teased Wanda, "Come and get it."

He hobbled towards her, hampered by the oversized clown shoes and his trousers coiled around his feet. She moved away as he got closer. She tossed the phony nose from hand to hand. She pretended that she was about to give it to him, and then snatched her hand away again as he reached for it. She tucked both hands behind her back, hiding the nose in her fist.

"You don't understand," Pindick stammered, "The nose is very important..."

"It's v-v-very important," mimicked Wanda, "Then you had better go and get it, hadn't you?" She stepped to the edge of the stage, and, to the horror of the clown, flung the little red nose into the audience.

The spectators got into the game at once, throwing the nose like a ball from one hand to another. Pindick pulled up his trousers, and clambered down the stairs at the apron into the dimly lit hall. From the balcony, the spotlight was pointed at him. He chased the nose, as the audience members transferred it from the front rows to the back of the house, and somehow or other, as the theater ushers got into the lark, it went out the back door, and Pindick followed his nose.

It was a spectacular exit, and the man-girl took a bow on the stage to thunderous applause.

His nose, as it turned out, would elude Pindick.

About an hour after the performance ended, the Dwarf Queen hammered on the door of Wanda's room.

"I can't find Pindy," she said, when Wanda came to the door. "He's not at the bar, he wasn't backstage, and he did not come back to our room."

"I know," Wanda replied, "He ran out of the back doors of the theater at the end of the scene, but then he was nowhere to be found."

"How was the show?"

"Hilarious. The audience loved it. So did I. He was a sensation."

"What made Pindy run out of the back of the theater? He has never done that before."

"Oh, my darling, you should have seen it," Wanda laughed, "He was chasing his nose."

"He lost his nose?"

"I took it off him."

The alabaster complexion of the Dwarf Queen seemed to turn a paler shade. "That nose is what puts him into his trance."

They heard the distant smash of glassware from the pool-deck bar. Someone started shouting in another language.

Wanda thought that the Dwarf Queen was about to faint. "You'd better explain."

"The sponge of the nose soaks up a special concoction which he inhales." She drew a sigh. "He is completely addicted to it." She was embarrassed to say the truth, so she spoke it quickly. "It's amyl nitrate, a little alcohol and some powder."

A gust of wind swept her black hair across her face.

There was a stamp of boots up the staircase.

Still in his circus wardrobe, the Ringmaster lumbered down the corridor. "There might be a problem."

"Do you know where Pindy is?"

"Jumba the giant said he saw Mr P running down to the beach. The wind caught his nose, and he chased after it."

They ran through the resort, with Wanda and the Dwarf Queen striding ahead, and the Ringmaster wheezing behind them, holding onto his top hat.

Jumba, the big muscle man, was standing on the sand barefoot and stripped to the waist, and his trousers were soaked. He was shivering, even though the night was warm. He had swum out into the treacherous backwash, but he had had no luck.

As the Dwarf Queen, the Ringmaster and the Man-girl approached, Jumba shook his head somberly. There was no sign of the clown in the water or anywhere down the beach, not even a footprint on the sand. There was no shadow under the moonlight. The four performers with their outlandish physiques stood in a frozen tableau, gazing into the tides, not sure what to do or feel or believe. Nobody moved, nobody dared to breathe a word.

But then, bobbing on the dark waves, they spotted the little red dot that was his nose. Jumba and the Ringmaster had to hold the Dwarf Queen back or she would have plunged into the breakers.

"Pindy! Pindy! Pindy!" wailed the Dwarf Queen, but it was only the blind moan of the wind, which offered any response.

Years after, when the Dwarf Queen was no longer welcome at the resort, they said that at the half-moon, you could still hear her voice on the whispers of the wind, calling, "Pindy, Pindy, Pindy."

Haunted by the black cloud of uncertainty, the circus lost its popularity without its star, and the resort fell on hard times, and the theater itself fell into disrepair after a bad winter storm damaged some of the wooden framework.

Every night, it was Pindick who closed the program; that was the grand finale. On the island, after that night, there were many who thought that it was the sad-faced clown who had had the last laugh, but, many believed that he had disappeared into the salty waters as if he had drowned in a sea of his own sorrowful tears.

Whatever happened to the clown after that remained a mystery. Eventually, the tales of his lively antics for a few short seasons faded from memory to legend, and, like all legends, nobody knew for certain if any of it ever existed. In the shrinking spotlight at the end, like the admirers watching his solo and like all jesters, everything vanished in a tiny pinhole. §

*Stuart Stromin is a South African-American writer
and filmmaker in Los Angeles*

9 7 9 8 8 8 5 9 6 1 9 0 5